A Comprehensive Guide to

Burglary and Robbery

2

Stephen Wade
and Stuart Gibbon

Straightforward Publishing
www.straightforwardco.co.uk

British cataloguing in Publication Data. A catalogue record is available for this book from the British library.

978-1-913342-50-0

Printed by 4edge Ltd www.4edge.co.uk
Cover design by BW Studio Derby

CONTENTS

INTRODUCTION

This book is a natural progression from our first two reference works, detailed below, and provides something we feel fills a gap on the shelf of the crime writer or reader. The aim was to provide a short guide which would deal with two specific subjects from both the police procedure viewpoint and from the position of a crime historian.

The rationale behind this is simple: the book provides a readable, lucid account of each subject in a manner very different from a book of law or a procedural manual. Students of legal history will want to read this in addition to the standard works, and the general reader will find here a mix of informed guidance on actual policing alongside some narratives of dramatic cases from history.

It is impossible in the space allowed to cover the entire historical development of criminal law in England of course, but we see the book as a starting-point, something to give a taster, as it were, while at the same time being thorough in the treatment of the subjects involved.

The Authors

Stephen Wade
Stephen's varied working life includes time in offices, on building sites and in retail clothing, but eventually he decided on teaching as a career and became a lecturer in English in further and higher education. In his last years

teaching at university, he was a part-time lecturer at Hull. After leaving his full-time posts, an opportunity came to work as a writer in residence in prisons, and he filled that role in three prisons, starting with a stretch of three years at Lincoln.

He became a crime historian after discovering an interest in local and social history, and after producing a number of books, he joined with Stuart on their works for readers and writers of crime, in both fact and fiction. Hence, Stephen is the historian and Stuart the professional detective. The aim in the historical material is to invite the reader to go further and deeper into the state of the law in years gone by.

In addition to his writing, Stephen acts as adviser to television productions on criminal matters, featuring in the BBC series *Murder Mystery and My Family,* and on Channel 5's *Inside Wormwood Scrubs.*

Stuart Gibbon

Stuart Gibbon travelled south from his native north-east to join the Metropolitan Police as a teenager. He successfully completed a tough 16 week training course at Peel Centre in Hendon and in September 1982 was posted to Wembley Division as Police Constable (PC) collar number 727. He worked as a uniformed response officer before becoming a detective and qualifying as a Sergeant. In the year 2000 he transferred to Lincolnshire Police where his career continued to develop. He served as a detective at every rank from Constable to Chief Inspector, during which time he became a Senior Investigating Officer (SIO) leading murder investigations. As a DCI he was seconded to the newly-formed East Midlands Special Operations Unit (EMSOU) as one of a small number of SIO's in charge of murder and kidnap throughout the five East Midlands police forces.

Following a career of more than 30 years Stuart made the decision to retire from the police service. He is now a writing consultant (GIB Consultancy) who advises authors to ensure their police procedures are accurate and authentic. He also appears on TV and radio as a policing expert and features in true crime documentaries about historical UK murder cases including *999:Killer on the line* and *Deadly Women*.

Our books

Our first book *The Crime Writer's Casebook* was published in December 2017. Although there are many true crime books in circulation, we believe that the *Casebook* is unique in that it looks at crime from both a historical and contemporary perspective. From the chaotic murder scenes of centuries past to the modern technology now used to track down the killer, the *Casebook* has proved hugely popular with the crime community, both writers and readers alike. If you're an aspiring or established writer looking to get your facts right then this book would be a useful addition to your bookshelf.

Book 2 *Being a Detective* is focused on the role of the UK detective, from the creation of the first professional detective department in 1842 to modern-day crime investigators. This book, published in March 2019, contains a wealth of information about the history and evolvement of the detective. Like its predecessor, *Being a Detective* contains true crime case studies and clear explanations for context. Summarised as *An A-Z Readers' and Writers' Guide to Detective Work Past and Present,* the book is presented in an alphabetical format with over 100 individual subject entries. From the **ABC principle** of crime investigation to **Zombie knife** this book is an essential companion for true crime fans.

The authors have now decided to look more closely at certain individual aspects of crime, the law and police procedure, with the publication of a series of comprehensive guides. These guides are intended to improve the readers' understanding of the subject area, whether criminal offences or the procedures involved during their investigation. They will provide you with a unique insight and take you behind the scenes to hear first-hand accounts from historical and modern-day policing.

Neither Stephen nor Stuart is a lawyer qualified in criminal law, but they both have considerable lifetime experience which enables them to speak with authority on the subject of true crime. The combination of a seasoned crime historian and an experienced former police detective will hopefully provide you with an interesting and informative read. They hope that you enjoy reading this guide and thank each and every one of you for your support.

Part 1

BURGLARY

"Thieves respect property; they merely wish the property to become theirs that they may more perfectly respect it."

G. K. Chesterton

Note: Names used for the practical examples are fictitious and bear no resemblance to persons current or historical except for the established classic cases included in the historical sections.

Introduction

In 1938, Geraldine Cadbury, J.P. as well as a writer, began her book on young offenders with this:

> *"One February day in 1814, at the Old Bailey sessions, five children were condemned to death – Fowler, aged 12 and Wolfe, aged 12, for burglary in a dwelling; Morris, age 8, Solomons, age 9 and Burrell, age 11, for burglary and stealing a pair of shoes."*

Such was once our attitude to burglary that we were prepared to issue a statute which would apply judicial killing to children. 'Burglary in a dwelling' at the time would have a fearful resonance.

Burglary is a crime with radically different effects, depending on *who* is burgled, and *how* they are burgled. The legal definition, basically referring to housebreaking in the hours of night (between 9 p.m. and 6 a.m.) was applied to the breaking and entering of a dwelling-house, with the added stipulation that there was an intent to commit a felony within the dwelling.

In the early phase of its use in law, it was bound up with a broad account of theft in general, and eventually came to have a specific meaning. Thanks to recent historical scholarship, the history of the concept has been subject to close examination. But for crime readers and crime writers it tends to be an offence that can thicken or complicate a storyline, as happens in reality (see the Maxwell Stewart/ Lincoln case below).

In crime writing, burglary really suggests the night, along

with invisible, stealthy, highly threatening actions by the deviants who wish ill to the good citizen. The burglar as a cultural figure is, on the one hand, a stereotype (that striped shirt and mask!) and yet the crime is unique, in that it cuts into sacred, sacrosanct areas of life – into the extremes of the personal.

All this was revised and changed by the 1968 Theft Act (dealt with by Stuart later). But the fundamental interest in burglary in the context of British culture and social life opens out into no end of areas of interest, as Eloise Moss, in her book, *Night Raiders*, (2019), has shown. She demonstrates very interestingly how themes such as property, alarm systems, insurance, literary influences and indeed protective laws, have all played a part in the history of the offence.

Our survey and guide offers insights into the offence through time, and also in the context of modern policing, where it is a complex notion. Overall, it goes back a very long way, to when it was a 'breech of a house' and that phrase says it all: something desperate, daring and unspeakably immoral, anti-society and anti-citizen.

Historical Perspectives

Note: legal terms used:
Felony: Any variety of criminal offence that, at common law, would entail a loss of land and goods – to the state.
Hundred: A division of a shire, probably formed some time in the 900s.

Pipe rolls: Accounts created and submitted to the Exchequer by a sheriff.

Tithing: A group of ten men, each of which would stand as security for the others. Hence investigations into offences was a communal concept.

Vills: A settlement which could be a tithing, a manor or a parish. Each would have its own court.

Back in Saxon times, in the centuries before the Norman Conquest of 1066, criminal matters were handled by two social creations: the *hundred* and the *tithing*. The hundred, a grouping of central importance, was responsible for choosing representatives who would organise and lead when it came to resolving disputes or settling on the guilty party in an offence. Even after 1066, these allocations still applied, before the radical changes of the thirteenth century, under Edward I, and later, in the reign of Henry II in particular. If a Norman was murdered, for instance, in the country after 1066, when the Saxons were the oppressed people, the leaders of the hundred would set about finding the culprit, and the result would often be a fee, a fine, paid. Matters were settled according to value.

In the early collections of laws from the English shires, such as Ethelbert, values were placed on goods or people harmed; as Christopher Hibbert put it, in his book, *The Roots of Evil*:

> *"The amount of compensation for offences committed on Sundays or holy days was double the ordinary rate, and by the laws of Alfred, a man who stole from a church had to suffer the additional penalty of the loss of a hand."*

Long before the word 'burglary' was conceived, the Saxons had the term *husbryce* (house-breech). Of course, the notion of the perpetrator also doing harm to someone was also there in the concept.

It was all linked to buildings and chattels owned. Consequently, in the years before the proper establishment of courts and the King's part in justice across the land, trial was often by ordeal or battle. The latter was not abolished until 1219 in England. The former entailed trials of strength and willpower in order to establish guilt or innocence. The ordeals might involve walking over red-hot ploughshares or reaching into boiling water to retrieve a stone at the bottom of a bowl. Whatever the case, such thinking is very odd when considered through modern eyes.

Burglary and robbery emerged when more people owned more; in the years before the reforms of Edward I and others, there was the added complexity of the sources of law. There was the long-established Roman Law, and there was the Canon Law of the church. These sat alongside what was shaped to become our English common law, and of course, for centuries, at the heart of this situation was the clash between church and state.

With this in mind, we may see the nature of the issues here: lords of manors had their courts, and bishops had their courts; on an everyday level, the hundreds dealt with minor offences, and alongside this sat the lesser church courts, which also dealt with matters of behaviour and morality in a given parish.

In other words, the notions of sin and crime interfused. Robbery, along with other serious crimes, was a sin primarily, and this demanded expiation. Hence, to see this in working practice, we only have to look at the pipe rolls or manorial rolls of early medieval manors to see that in most cases, fines were exacted, and of course, penance required.

Burglary emerged as a clearer transgression by the fifteenth century. From that point onwards, in the general social history of Britain, there was a steady expansion of the commercial interest and of course, later, of empire. Increasingly up to modern times, burglary is all about night – fear and protection of what one has. In 1940, for instance, in a handbook printed for use by special constables, we have this:

BUILDINGS (Vulnerable)

'*When patrolling a section, a Special Constable should endeavor to make himself fully acquainted with all important property thereon, especially vulnerable property – property which is likely to be attacked by the criminally minded. Such property should be thoroughly examined when the occupants are away, such as at night or closing times.*'

From Medieval to Georgian

It was in the reign of Henry II that a radical revision of the legal system took place. Henry reigned 1154–1189, and from the 1170s he began the establishment of what became the assize courts, in which the king's justices travelled around the land, holding courts which could last perhaps for several weeks, and in that time they heard all varieties of cases.

When Henry returned from some time in France, part of the empire then, he realised that clerics had been committing serious crimes and receiving only penance or supposed fines. The church courts were hardly, he saw, any central concept, and what was needed was a universal, national structure of courts. From the early medieval times, the proliferation of courts (hundreds, vills, church etc.) had made hearings (and justice) difficult for the less wealthy. There were cases in which people had followed the king around the empire, waiting for a chance to have him hear their case and make a judgment.

There had also been Norman law since the invasion of William I, and it had become clear to Henry that law in England should be derived from English life, morals, customs and social functions. In other words, the common law, from precedents and from former judgments, ought to be fundamental, and should be something to build on, through the work of the justices.

The king was not alone in this: there were learned men such as Ranulf Glanville, who wrote a work which became a sort of text-book on common law: the *Tractatus de legibus et consuetudinibus regni Angliae (*Treatise on the laws and customs of the realm of England). A real landmark in Henry's work was in 1176 when, at the Assize of Northampton, the six circuits were established – the regions and court centres at which the courts would meet. The justices would represent the king: their justice was his justice.

Serious offences such as murder, rape, robbery and arson, would now be heard, and within these cases, there would be thefts which would later be called 'burglary.' Basically, every kind of offence covered by the word 'robbery' would now be heard and discussed. But there was no actual offence relating to breaking into property until later, in the mid-fifteenth century. At that time, breaking into a building with an intent to steal was becoming more markedly identified. But there were features of the concept, such as the fact that the building in question had to be occupied at the time of the house-breach, and it had to be a nocturnal break-in.

A house break-in during the day, it was later established, would simply be a variety of *trespass*. This has one definition that applies in this context: 'An action brought for injury done to person or property with violence... when done as part of an unwarrantable entry upon land of the plaintiff.'

By the eighteenth century, and the emergence of the 'Bloody Code' the notion of protecting property had become a very different legal entity. One's land and dwelling-place was a focal concept in English life and identity. Through the Middle Ages, there had been a 'watch and ward' at night, after town gates were shut. There were constables later, who would be a 'night watch.' But by the eighteenth-century things had changed totally.

The Bloody Code was a collection of laws which were intended to protect homes and wealth, as well as people and moveable property. This collection of statutes formed a numerous set of laws which were classified as capital offences, and this was not revised until the 1820s.

From the records of the Old Bailey we can look at a case from the period of the Bloody Code. In 1730 for instance, Elizabeth Hickman was indicted for burglary, having allegedly broken into the house of Thomas Lovet, where she stole goods to the value of over six guineas. She had entered by a sash-window; she had gone through to the home in question from next door. She was found the morning after, with most of the goods apparently gone, though she had over a guinea on her person. She was acquitted of a burglary, but had committed a felony (theft). She was transported for seven years.

In contrast, how different matters were when there was

violence involved. In Roscommon, 1820, Stephen McGarry was on trial charged with "burglary, with intent to commit a robbery, and there were further details: 2nd indictment, demanding money; 3rd indictment, for breaking into the dwelling house of Michael Hannully after sunset and injuring the same; 4th indictment, for forcibly exacting money; 5th indictment, the same with intent to rob; 6th indictment, for appearing by night, armed." He was destined for the gallows.

TWO CASE STUDIES

A closer look at several case studies, one from 1303 and one from the early twentieth century will prove to be enlightening.

1303–1305 Richard of Pudlicott

In 1915, T. F. Tout, a Professor of History at the University of Manchester, gave a lecture on 'A Medieval Burglary' at the John Rylands Library. This was subsequently published, and what was revealed was a rare insight into the security (or lack of it) in the administration of the royal Wardrobe Treasury at Westminster Abbey. The ruler at the time was Edward I, and as he was absent from London in 1303, Richard of Pudlicott, a wool merchant, with a gang of rogues, decided to steal a massive hoard of coins and plate from the treasury.

This happened in April 1303, when Edward found himself deeply in debt, and he was levying taxes very heavily. But at the time of this crime, the king had had to go north and try to conquer the rebel Scots. In London there was an establishment of legal and administrative centres, the core of the king's control of his realm. Notably, the Court of Common Pleas was there, and the office of Chancery; at the heart of the royal secretariat was the King's Wardrobe, an outfit that did far more than simply look after the royal clothes, as the name suggests.

Prof. Tout explains, "...the king's wardrobe had become an organised office of government. Its clerks rivalled the officers of the Exchequer in their dealings with financial matters, and the officers of the Chancery, in the numbers of letters, mandates, orders and general administrative business which passed through their hands."

But in April 1303, the king and all his main servants had removed to York, always the focus of operations when the forces of the country were taking on the Scots. Back in Westminster, there was a total lack of organisation – and of security.

The man who should have been in charge of security in London was John Shenche, the keeper of the king's palace. He was also the keeper of the Fleet prison on the Thames bank. It was common practice, for centuries, for men in favour to hold multiple offices, some of them sinecures, and corruption was built into the system, with nepotism at the very core. Perhaps his mind was on other things, but whatever he did or did not do, the fact is that Richard of Pudlicott saw an opportunity to enact a grand theft. Discipline was relaxed. The officers of the Abbey, known as the *obedientiaries*, were of no use at all, and while the king was away, there were parties and a general neglect of order and security.

T. F. Tout describes the beginning of the theft: "The very day after the king left Westminster, Pudlicott found a ladder reared up against a house near the palace gates. He put this ladder up against one of the palace windows of the chapter-house; he climbed up the ladder; found a window that opened by means of a cord; opened the window and swung himself by the same cord into the chapter-house." From there he went to the refectory and grabbed all the silver plate.

Richard then went for the treasury of the king; the crypt under the chapter house had become a store for valuables, and we know that there were such items as coins there, and silver was the only metal at the time used by the mint, so we know the nature of the booty. Prof Tout explains the method of burglary, as the crypt was very deep and the walls extremely thick: "... masons and carpenters were called in, so that some breaking in of the structure was attempted, and in particular it suggests that the churchyard was the thoroughfare through which the robbers moved their booty."

Of course, Richard could not expect to get away with this. Strangely, items from the hoard were found all over London; scores of people were charged with the offence when the king returned, and monks were involved. The monks who should have been in charge – the obedientiaries, were seen as largely culpable. Many of them were hanged.

One line of thought about how the masonry work was covered over is that some hemp was grown over the place where the walls were breached. Prof Tout opines that "... half the neighbours must have been cognizant of, if not participating in, the crime."

The king, still in Scotland, ordered an investigation, led by John Droxford. There was a long investigation, and not until 1305, when matters north were settled and Edward was back at home did the whole affair come to a conclusion, with Richard of Pudlicott being sent to the gallows. Much of the lost treasure was recovered. Prof Tout gives a helpful summing-up of the men of this tumultuous time. He wrote that "Shining virtues and gross vices stood side by side."

What the Pudlicott case tells us about burglary, long before it was really isolated and defined, is that it was a very easy matter, in a world without a police force, well locked buildings and any real system of property protection – even in the life of the sovereign.

John Vickers, 1776

This case is one of thousands of a similar nature: burglaries committed by a gang of roughs, and on vulnerable people.

John Vickers, a true renegade and worry to all good people, was born in Hemsworth back Moor, but went on the rampage around his own area in Sheffield around midnight on February 11, 1775. He was out to steal and take away everything he could, however small. First, he joined up with a man called John Booth and they stole money (including a bad shilling), along with mutton and half a pound of butter, from John Murfin, whose home was near the Blue Ball public house. Vickers was clearly the leading light in a fairly large band of villains around the area, and he wasn't satisfied with the first nocturnal foray into the homes of peaceful citizens.

He went out again, this time with three other men, and his target then was anyone who might happen to come out of the local hostelries the worse for drink. But his luck was out that time, because one of the intended victims was a man who knew Vickers. He was, in fact, a former employer in the days when Vickers had been an apprentice. Before that, Vickers and his gang had also robbed John Staniforth of money, mutton, sugar and flax. Again, they located a spot near a public house to attack – this time, the Glass House.

Vickers was soon tracked down now that the law had a name. He was soon at York, along with Booth, facing two indictments in front of a grand jury. The facts of his robberies on both Murfin and Staniforth were then ascertained. Booth was acquitted, but Vickers had the death sentence on him. Mr Justice Gould put on the black cap and spoke the terrible words with the phrase 'hanged by the neck' in the familiar few sentences. Vickers was indeed hanged, at the Tyburn on 30 March 1776.

The case demonstrates, as happens so often, that transgressions tend to be more complex when there are participants known in the community and known to each other; so often a local narrative opens out into enmity, oppositions and intrusions which are evident in the way a community functions. The intimate geography of a locality carries with it a profound depth of feeling, of emotions, so often found at the very core of a violent crime.

From Victorian to Modern

Burglary in the nineteenth and early twentieth centuries was a very different beast to that of the earlier times. The reasons for this are not hard to find. The industrial revolution brought the expansion of towns and cites; in the wake of this there was more private property; from that we have material wealth, and where there are people who own material wealth, there are burglars and thieves.

After the establishment of the first proper police force in 1829, and then the first professional detective force in

1842, there was some help at hand for people who had been victims of burglary and of larceny or any other variety of theft. But of course, the incidence of crime remained high. There were extremes of rich and poor in London, admirably described by Charles Dickens in *Oliver Twist* for example, there were frequent street robberies, and of course, there were plenty of burglaries. The night was still the time when citizens were at their most vulnerable.

As the urban areas expanded and the police forces in the regions were gradually formed and regulated, throughout the mid to later Victorian period, burglary became a much more 'visible' offence in the sense of wider and more dramatic reporting. After all, a burglar is someone who enters your property under cover of darkness, someone who prowls and stealthily steals your belongings, or even worse, the burglar may have designs on your person too. You are helpless within your own walls, and after all, 'The Englishman's home is his castle.'

In the pages of the *Illustrated Police News* and in popular newspapers, tales of burglars became common, and were often highly dramatised. The infamous criminal Charles Peace, hanged for murder in 1879, was also a skilled burglar. He operated his nocturnal thefts around London. He was arrested in Blackheath during a burglary on 10 October 1878, and he was to become an almost mythic figure in popular culture.

But in a more everyday criminal affair, a case such as one reported from Bradford in 1869 is more typical. *The Illustrated Police News* used the headline, "A thief in a bedroom at Bradford" and the report was worded in such a way as to convey the peculiar fears associated with the crime: "Every homeowner's worst nightmare came true for Mrs Cockin in the Manningham area of Bradford....she heard a rustling and woke to find an intruder attempting to scramble under the bed..."

By the twentieth century, there is the emergence of the term 'cat burglar' which signifies the alarming sneakiness and stealth of the actions involved in the crime. A typical report, like thousands of others, is this from 1926:

"Cat Burglary, Jewellery worth £1,600 stolen, Flat entered in family's absence. A cat burglar last night stole jewellery valued at £1,600 from a flat in Maida vale, London. He gained entry by using a stack pipe, and from the bedroom of Mr D. E. Nario Barros took the jewellery, including a graduated pearl necklace. The burglary took place while the family were out..."

This has all the features of the crime. Valuables were taken when nobody was home, and the theft took place in the most private and intimate space – the bedroom.

Along with burglary came all the other twentieth century businesses linked to protection: insurance, domestic alarms and various devices added to building techniques. The notion of 'defensible space' became a popular topic in the 1960s and later. In short, burglary had become the crime which reached into the very heart of our personal lives – except, of course, until the advent of the internet and of mobile phones.

In the twentieth century, burglars and burglary were often represented in fiction and in non-fiction as somehow comic and ridiculous figures. A typical instance of this is in a novel by the writer and barrister Henry Cecil, who has a scene in his novel, *No Bail for the Judge* in which a homeowner arrives home to find a burglar.

This follows:

> *"'What the dickens are you doing in here?'*
> *... Elizabeth had never met a burglar before, but she could*
> *not help admiring his cheek. Moreover, he did not sound or*
> *look as though he were likely to attack her. He remained*
> *quietly by the safe. Her courage started to return and she*
> *began to think of the episode as an interesting one to be*
> *developed..."*

This hardly stands up to a reality test. But it made good fiction at the time.

TWO CASE STUDIES
On a Rampage

John Freeman, Charles Metcalfe and Henry Coates, on 20 March 1807, went on a rampage, and it was a fatal mistake These three Brigg labourers decided that they would grab some easy money by breaking into a house at Rye Hill, Killingholme in January of this year.

They took a large amount of cash and a gold watch. But another man called Granger informed on them and went free. The whole escapade was partly daring and partly farcical. Metcalfe knew the place as he had worked for the owner at one time, and the gang decided to play around and pretend to be various people in disguise.

They dressed in all kinds of clothes and even wore false beards; but there the farce ended, because they were armed. Ironically, Granger, who escaped with his neck in the end, made them swear an oath. The story later told was that Granger urged them to the deed, even though some were not so enthusiastic when the fantasy turned into reality.

When they did enter the house, a fight followed, and Mrs Fox gave a good account of herself; a shot was fired, but no-one was hurt.

After the attack and theft, the news was spread across the county and over the Humber, and so they were all found at various places and arrested. What emerged was that they had been the gang who had done other robberies across that area for some time. Naturally, when all the tales were told in court and it looked as though Granger, who was acquitted, was the leading light of the gang, there were problems. The man seems to have known all the moves and ploys that would get him through, notably serving in the army, and indeed the last we hear of him is that he was in the army, on the Isle of Wight.

The scene of the multiple hanging was, of course, very moving: one was a family man, and Metcalfe was emotionally wrecked. The usual final speeches followed and the only concession made by the authorities was that their bodies were not sent for dissection.

Maxwell-Stewart, 1925

This case, which is principally recorded as a trial for murder, ended in an incredibly severe sentence for burglary. It concerns a burglary on a private home in Trowbridge just before Christmas, 1925. Charles Richards made enough noise to awaken his friend Walter Stourton in the early hours of Christmas Eve. Stourton found his friend downstairs, mortally wounded from gunshots, and the man died a short time later in hospital. What emerged was a burglary gone horribly wrong, as both Richards, and the two robbers, his assailants, were armed.

Maxwell Stewart and his friend, John Lincoln, planned to

enter the Stourton home (of which Richards was landlord) and steal cash and valuables. It was well known around the area that Richards carried cash and that he was armed. The attackers therefore took guns from the store in their barracks, as they were soldiers in the Royal Horse Artillery. They were armed with distinctive marks on barrels and in the internal workings, where slight damage was done when the guns were fired. The ballistics was excellent, and also, the events of the fateful night's burglary were soon put together.

Police soon assembled a sequence of events. There were empty beer-bottles found, and nearby in a field, there was evidence of people being located. Clearly the two soldiers had watched and waited, then entered the home, and there was Richards, armed and ready to defend his property. Richards had an arrangement with his tenant that the back door would be open at certain times, and Richards was inside when the attackers came.

John Lincoln was found guilty of murder and hanged at Shepton Mallet prison by Thomas Pierrepoint in March 1926. He was only 23 years old. The defence had been that Lincoln shot in a panic when confronted by the armed Richards, and that his shot in response led to an accidental death, and so manslaughter was argued, to no avail. There was not enough evidence to convict Maxwell Stewart, but he was in for a shock.

T. E. H. Jervis, writing about the case in 1937, describes the movements of Lincoln on the fatal night:

"... after leaving the guard-room he went to his barrack room where he was seen by one of his five bed-fellows to change his clothing, borrow a fellow gunner's raincoat

and take what appeared to be a torch...there were several small incidents in the morning after the murder which taken together, required explanation. When jokingly asked where he had been the previous night, he did not deny being absent, but said, 'Keep quiet... this may be serious for me.'... when the murder was being discussed, he remarked, 'I hope the police don't find out I had a revolver.'"

All the burglars' actions were easily traced, and the trial came up at the assizes. But there was no unanimous verdict. Then comes the next event in the story. Maxwell Stewart had also committed burglary and the trial for that offence was heard at Salisbury Assizes in May 1926. Constable Jervis again explains:

"... he pleaded guilty, hoping, perhaps, as a last resort, that he might therefore receive a mitigation of sentence. But he was disappointed. He received what must be the record sentence for burglary 'with intent' of fourteen years penal servitude...The most that can be said of him is that he was influenced throughout by a stronger character than himself."

As we look at the offence of burglary through history, nothing informs us more regarding the differences in how they were perceived than the failure of a bill to pass into law in 1821, when there was a push to have burglary removed as a capital offence.

Contemporary

If you're a reader or writer of crime the offence of burglary may well interest you at some point. I think it's important to have some basic knowledge of the relevant law as well as examples for context. I'm also going to explain the police response to an allegation of burglary and how a typical criminal investigation into a burglary may be carried out.

Police services in the UK tend to investigate and manage crime in different ways, from the initial response to the way that the investigation is conducted, so it would be very difficult for me to provide individual approaches for each force. I can, however, give you a good understanding and guide you through the process of what is likely to happen. If you're writing about a particular 'genuine' police force and you need specific information, such as the name of a unit/department or other details, then I would advise you to initially research that force via the internet or social media. The information you are looking for may be available to the public. You could also contact the force directly, explaining the information you require and the reason you need it. They may be happy to share information with you (this will very much depend on the type of information) and answer your questions. I would suggest that you initially contact the force media/press office who may be able to point you in the right direction. The response to your enquiry will probably vary from force to force, but I have known some forces that have been extremely helpful to writers, providing a tour of the police station and access to police officers, so don't be afraid to ask.

The law

Burglary is a criminal offence which is covered by Section 9 of the Theft Act 1968. There are two different forms of burglary which are known as Sections 9(1)(a) and 9(1)(b). The former requires proof that a person entered a building with specific intent and the latter relates to the actions of a person who has already entered a building. I'm going to show you the law as written in the statute books, then explain it in simplistic terms.

Burglary – Theft Act 1968 Section 9(1)(a)

(1) A person is guilty of burglary if –

(a) he enters any building or part of a building as a trespasser and with intent to commit any offence mentioned in subsection (2) below...

(2) The offences referred to above are offences of stealing anything in the building or part of the building, inflicting on any person therein any grievous bodily harm and of doing unlawful damage to the building or anything therein.

In a nutshell, if someone goes into a building without permission intending to either steal something, seriously assault (GBH) someone or cause criminal damage (or any combination of the three) they commit burglary under Section 9(1)(a). The wording of the offence states that they are guilty of burglary, a term normally reserved for a court of law, which simply means that they have committed the offence of burglary. You may also have noticed that the wording relates to 'he' entering any building (a term common throughout criminal law), but of course, burglary can be committed by a woman too. Certain types of distraction burglary are often committed by women, either alone or as part of a team (see distraction burglary).

The intention of the burglar to steal, GBH or damage refers to the time when they actually entered the building, rather than before or after, for the offence to have been committed. The term 'steal' simply means an intention to commit theft (Section 1 Theft Act 1968). This covers most things with the exception of electricity (which is not classed as 'property' for the purposes of theft) and taking a conveyance (a car etc.) which is a separate criminal offence.

Section 9(1)(a) – Example 1
Smith has a string of previous convictions for dishonesty. During the festive period he targets unoccupied houses to steal Christmas presents which he sells to obtain the money to buy drugs. He visits a house in darkness and knocks on the door to check that no-one is home. He looks through the window and sees a pile of gifts underneath the Christmas tree which he is planning to steal. He goes around the back of the house, forces the patio door and enters. He steals a number of wrapped gifts together with some cash and jewellery. He had the intention to steal when he entered the building as a trespasser and has committed Section 9(1)(a) burglary.

Example 2
Roberts is owed £500 by Gibson following a previous game of poker. Roberts has asked for the money on several occasions and has threatened Gibson with violence if he doesn't pay him, to no avail. Roberts finds out where Gibson lives, arms himself with a kitchen knife, and goes to his house. His intention is to cause Gibson serious harm to teach him a lesson. When Roberts arrives at the address, he kicks the front door in and runs inside looking for Gibson.

He had the intention to cause Grievous Bodily Harm (GBH) to Gibson when he entered the building as a trespasser and has committed Section 9(1)(a) burglary.

Burglary – Theft Act 1968 Section 9(1)(b)

(1) A person is guilty of burglary if –

(b) having entered any building or part of a building as a trespasser he steals or attempts to steal anything in the building or that part of it or inflicts or attempts to inflict on any person therein any grievous bodily harm.

The second part of burglary, which is covered by Section 9(1)(b), doesn't require the same intent on entry as 9(1)(a) and is limited to the offences of theft, GBH and attempts to commit those two offences. There is no reference to causing unlawful damage in this second part of the Act. Unlike the reference to GBH in 9(1)(a) which is limited to an offence of Wounding or GBH with intent (Section 18 Offences Against the Person Act 1861), Section 9(1)(b) includes Wounding or Inflicting GBH (Section 20 Offences Against the Person Act 1861) which doesn't require proof of intent, as well as the Section 18 GBH offence.

This type of burglary involves a person's behaviour after entering a building as a trespasser. If a person hid in the public area of a shop during opening hours until the shop closed, then they would not have technically committed an offence under this part of the Act as they didn't enter the shop as a trespasser. However, if they then moved to another part of the building (e.g. storeroom), then they would be a trespasser and would commit 9(1)(b) burglary.

Section 9(1)(b) – Example
Faulkner goes for a drink in the Kings Arms public house

with a friend. During the evening he decides to hide in the public toilets of the pub until closing time as he is trying to avoid another customer in the bar. He later emerges from the toilets to find that the pub has closed and is now empty and locked. At this point he decides to break into the gaming machines in the bar lounge in order to steal the money inside them. He smashes a machine open and is about to remove the money inside when he is disturbed by the landlord who detains him. Faulkner became a trespasser when he left the toilets and entered the lounge after closing time. Knowing that the pub was shut he then decided to try to steal the contents of the gaming machine and as he broke into the machine, having entered a part of a building (lounge) as a trespasser and having attempted to steal, he has committed Section 9(1)(b) burglary.

Entry

The legislation which covers burglary (Theft Act 1968) doesn't define the term 'entry' so its meaning is left to case law and the decision of the criminal courts. Most of the time it will be quite obvious whether a person has actually entered a building, but not in every case. In the case of R v Davis (1823) a small boy was observed pushing his finger against a pane of glass in a window which fell inside the jewellery shop. The forepart of the boy's finger could be seen on the inside of the shop by the owner. The jury convicted the boy of burglary and, although the Judge had some concerns at the time as to whether this constituted sufficient entry for the offence of burglary, the Judges agreed that it did and the conviction stood.

The current approach to the term 'entry' is reflected in R v Brown (1975) where the defendant broke a shop window and leant in through the hole while reaching inside to try to steal the contents. His lower half remained outside the shop. He was arrested and convicted of burglary, but then appealed against his conviction on the basis that he had not actually 'entered' the building. His conviction stood because the Court of Appeal ruled that entry needed to be either 'effective' or 'substantial' and in this case it was considered to have been 'effective' making the offence of burglary complete. Entry could still be 'effective' even if the defendant didn't enter the premises with his whole body and as he had entered with intent to steal his appeal against conviction for burglary was dismissed.

At common law, the insertion of an instrument would constitute entry as long as the instrument was inserted to enable the offence of burglary to take place. So, a hook on the end of a pole used to steal items from near the door/window or a gun pointed through an open letterbox with the intention of causing GBH would both apply. On the other hand, if the instrument had been inserted merely to help gain entry, such as the use of a coat hanger to pick a lock, then this would not be considered as entry for the purposes of the Act.

Trespasser

As with the term 'entry' whether a person is a trespasser will often be quite obvious. If they force entry to a building when they have no right to be there or walk into a property when uninvited, then they will most likely be trespassing. There will be occasions though when a person may have a general permission to enter a building or part of a building for a legitimate purpose, but their true intention is to steal or commit one of the other specified offences. As these intentions form no part of the permission to enter (in other words the owner would not have allowed entry were the actual intentions clear) the person would become a trespasser from the moment they entered the building and would commit burglary.

Example
Morris lives in a large house with several bedrooms. He has given a key to Wade and told him that he can go in whenever he likes to sleep in one of the bedrooms. One night Wade uses the key to let himself into the house. Rather than sleeping there he intends to steal a new camera which Morris has recently bought. In these circumstances Wade has committed a burglary under Section 9(1)(a) as Morris clearly didn't give him the key to the house so that he could steal from him. Any intention to steal (GBH or damage) voids the general permission given to enter.

Building
In order to commit a burglary there must be entry to a building or part of a building. For the purposes of the Act a building is generally considered to be a structure of a permanent nature although a substantial portable structure could possibly be classed as a building. A case in point is B&S v Leathley (1979) where the defendants entered a freezer container in a farmyard and stole goods from it. The container was resting on railway sleepers, weighed three tons and was twenty-five foot long. It hadn't been moved for over two years, had a door and locks, and was connected to the mains electricity supply. A charge of burglary was appealed to the Crown Court who ruled that the container was a 'building' for the purposes of the Theft

Act 1968 as it was a structure likely to remain in place for the foreseeable future. The appeal was rejected and the conviction for burglary stood.

Tents and marquees fall outside the term 'building' even if it is someone's home but inhabited vehicles and vessels (such as house boats or motor homes) can be considered a 'building' for the purposes of burglary.

Categories of burglary

The police will take details and record the crime as a burglary-dwelling or burglary non-dwelling. Sometimes these categories are referred to as burglary-residential or non-residential. The category of the crime needs to be correct to ensure that the appropriate investigation is carried out and to assist statistical analysis of burglary offences. For many years a garage attached to a house (with no integral door leading into the house), a garden shed and other structures within the boundaries of the property have been recorded as burglary non-dwelling, but a recent change in the Home Office guidelines means that these types of crimes are now recorded as burglary-dwelling. This change has led to an increase of recorded burglary-dwelling offences and an amended category of burglary-business and community for all other burglary types.

Examples

The police are called to a private house which has been broken into whilst the occupiers have been away on holiday. They have returned to find that the rear door has been forced and a number of electrical items have been stolen. This crime should be recorded by the police as a burglary-residential.

A member of the public who lives in a flat above some shops calls police due to the sound of an alarm nearby in the early hours of the morning. The police arrive to find that the front window of a mobile phone shop has been broken and a number of phone handsets have been stolen. This crime should be recorded as a burglary-business and community.

I'm going to explain how the police actually record details to create a crime and what action they should take at the scene in due course, but firstly let's look at what will happen when the report of a burglary is received by the police.

Police response

If you phone the police to report a burglary you will be put through to the local Force Control Room (FCR). These rooms, quite often at or near the local force Headquarters, are the focal point of communications for the force. They contain a mixture of civilian police staff and police officers who receive telephone calls from the public and communicate with the police officers/staff on the street via radio. You will be asked to supply your details and a summary of what has happened. This is so that the 'call-taker' can make an assessment of any risk to the public and attending officers. Any descriptions of people involved, vehicles and direction of travel can prove crucial if the burglary has recently happened. The call will be given a unique reference number and a record of the incident will be created by the call-taker on their computer. Incidents are given a consecutive number which is used in conjunction with the date running from midnight to 2359 hours each day (the first incident created on 4/1/20 will be referred to as Incident 1 of 4/1/20 and so on throughout the day).

The incident number will often be quoted by police when they appeal for witnesses in the media.

Example
Police are appealing for witnesses to a burglary which took place on Friday 13th December 2019 at about 3.00am. The O2 mobile phone shop in High Street was entered and a number of mobile phones were stolen. A red car was seen in the area shortly before the burglary. Police are asking for any witnesses or anyone with information in relation to the burglary to contact the investigating officer DC Gibbon via 101 quoting Incident number 27 of 13/12/19.

Police incidents are graded as one of three categories: Urgent, Priority or Routine depending on the circum-stances and the information supplied to the call-taker. A report of a burglary may be graded as Urgent if the crime is in progress or an offender has recently been disturbed at the scene. It may also be graded as Urgent if violence has been used or threatened. In other circumstances a report of a burglary is likely to be graded as either Priority or Routine.

The FCR will allocate an officer to attend the report of a burglary. This person will usually be a uniformed police constable (PC) or sometimes a police community support officer (PCSO). Depending on the time of day and force resources, they may be walking or driving alone when the incident is allocated to them. If the burglary has recently happened or the person(s) responsible could be nearby, then other units may also attend to assist their colleagues and carry out a search of the local area. The officers are likely to be in uniform and driving a marked police vehicle.

They will inform the FCR by radio when they have arrived at the scene and provide an update on the situation as soon as possible.

The actions of the first police to attend the scene of a burglary are very important, regardless of the circumstances. They are sometimes referred to as 'reporting officer' which may suggest that their role is simply to record the details and move on to the next call. Nothing could be further from the truth. The first officer to attend the scene of any crime has a vital role to play in making sure that evidence is secured and preserved. The actions taken or not taken by them will have an impact on the success of any future investigation. The first officer on scene will become the 'initial investigating officer' for that crime until the case is handed over to another officer, which may or may not happen, depending on the circumstances.

The initial investigating officer will gather as much information as possible from the victim and any witnesses. They will prepare and submit a crime report and may record a witness statement if appropriate. For many years both would involve paper forms being handwritten, but with the introduction of improved police equipment it is more than likely that they would now be completed electronically using the officer's Blackberry or similar device. The victim would be supplied with a unique crime report number to assist with future police contact and insurance purposes if appropriate.

Details of property stolen, together with descriptions and identifying features (serial numbers, property marking), should be obtained as soon as possible. The police encourage the public to mark TV's, computers and other electrical items by writing their house number and full postcode on the rear of the item using an ultra-violet (UV) pen. This identifies the property item as belonging to a specific address and helps the police to trace the owner should the property come into their possession.

The initial investigating officer should also take a walk around the immediate area to check for evidential opportunities. These may include witnesses at neighbouring or overlooking properties, CCTV which may have captured the burglary and/or offenders and property which may have been discarded nearby. They should carry out house to house enquiries and note the results of those enquiries, even where negative or no reply.

The first officer to attend the scene should also make an assessment in relation to any forensic opportunities which may be available and make sure that the scene is secured and preserved where appropriate. This may include arranging for the property to be boarded-up if the owners can't be contacted, making sure that any broken glass which may contain fingerprints isn't disposed of before being examined or protecting any footwear marks left by the offenders. They should also make arrangements for the attendance of a Crime Scene Investigator (CSI) in cases where the burglary fits the criteria for such attendance (the majority of residential burglaries should be attended by CSI, but burglaries at shops and other commercial premises may not).

As you can see, the first officer to attend the scene of a burglary isn't just expected to record details of the crime, but has a number of responsibilities which, if carried out effectively, are likely to improve the chances of a successful investigation.

Police investigation

The investigating officer for a burglary will depend on the type of burglary and the circumstances. Residential burglaries are usually investigated by a detective who may be part of a team tasked with investigating such crimes or from a general CID office with a varied workload. It's likely that the officer will be a Detective Constable (DC) although, on occasion, it could be a Detective Sergeant (DS). Detectives may also investigate some commercial burglaries at business premises if they are of high-value, involve violence or are believed to be part of a series of similar crimes which may benefit from specialist investigation. The majority of commercial burglaries are investigated by uniformed officers (PC's) who will have a varied workload and will normally have to manage their investigations around their shift patterns.

Every burglary investigation has its own unique characteristics, but there are some consistent 'lines of enquiry' which are likely to be considered by the police during each case. They may not all be relevant to every crime of burglary, but will form part of an investigative template which officers are encouraged to follow.

House to house enquiries

Local enquiries in the vicinity of the burglary are very important and the sooner these are carried out the better. In an ideal world, the first officer to attend the scene should try to speak with neighbours to see if they were in at the time and can provide any useful information. It could be that someone has seen something which appears relatively innocent, such as a person knocking on doors in the area. This could prove to be important as the investigation progresses as that person could be a witness or indeed the suspect. The investigating officer needs to make sure that house to house enquiries are carried out at appropriate locations where anyone may have seen or heard anything suspicious. The results of these enquiries, negative or otherwise, should be recorded on the computerised crime report relating to that burglary. If any witnesses are identified as a result of these enquiries, then a written witness statement should be taken from them to assist the investigation. House to house enquiries are key to a burglary investigation.

Closed circuit television (CCTV)

The quantity and quality of CCTV systems is now far greater that it's ever been and has led to CCTV evidence playing a critical role in criminal investigations. There are different types of CCTV, all of which could be relevant to a burglary investigation. These include local authority (council), commercial properties (business) and private (houses). Police are likely to know where the local authority cameras are positioned in their area, but probably won't know about others. This is another reason why it's important for the officer dealing with the burglary to walk around the immediate area to look for the presence of any cameras which may have recorded evidence. They would then need to find out who the camera(s) belonged to and obtain the consent of that person to view the footage as soon as possible. A lot of CCTV systems record over footage after a certain period of time which could result in a loss of evidence, so time is of the essence. Once the relevant footage has been viewed, regardless of whether it contains anything of use, it should be copied onto a portable disc (DVD/CD) and retained by the police for any future prosecution of the case. The disc will be taken to the police station where it should be securely stored.

If the suspect(s) involved in a burglary is captured on CCTV the investigating officer will arrange for still images to be printed from the footage. If the identity of those responsible isn't known, these images will be circulated by the local Intelligence Unit to see if local officers recognise them. They may also be circulated to other stations and Forces if it is thought that they may be travelling criminals from another area. Even if the suspect is trying to conceal their identity by wearing a hooded top or other face-covering, it may be possible to identify them through their clothing, particularly if it's distinctive and recovered by police.

CASE STUDIES – CCTV
A serial caravan burglar in Wales, described as a 'one man crime wave', was caught on CCTV raiding a mobile home by the owner who was on holiday in another country at the time. The burglar had already entered a woman's mobile home while she was sleeping and stole a power washer, headphones and a large amount of cigarettes. As he entered another caravan the owner received an alert on his mobile phone and was able to view the burglary as it took place on his CCTV, despite being on holiday in Spain at the time. The sophisticated system allowed the owner to watch 'live' footage of his caravan even though he was more than 1000 miles away. The burglar was identified from the footage and subsequently arrested. He had been due to go on trial at Mold Crown Court for three caravan burglaries and two counts of theft, but pleaded guilty to the offences and was jailed for two years.

Two men from the Yorkshire area were convicted of burglary despite attempts to vandalise the CCTV at the scene of the crime. John Marshall and Sam Cosgrove caused £2,500 worth of damage to the surveillance cameras and their server at a flour mill near Goole, but were unable to stop the cameras recording their actions as they cut wires on the roof and inside the building. They were also heard on the audio recording of the CCTV hitting a reinforced window with a rock and one of them was heard to call the other "Jonathan". Police officers recognised the pair from the CCTV footage and they were arrested. Both men pleaded guilty to burglary due to the strength of the evidence against them. Marshall was jailed for 2 years and 10 months and Cosgrove was given a community order with a financial penalty. The investigating police officer commented, "This was a fast-moving investigation which was assisted greatly thanks to the quality CCTV footage and local knowledge of our officers which pinned both Cosgrove and Marshall to the crime".

Forensic evidence

Not all burglaries are examined by Crime Scene Investigator's (CSI) as most forces have limited resources and policies in relation to crime scene attendance. Residential burglaries should receive a visit from a CSI, but it may be that some commercial burglaries do not. It will often depend on the circumstances and the likelihood of the recovery of forensic evidence such as fingerprints and/or DNA from the scene. If a person has been arrested in relation to a burglary, then a CSI is likely to attend the burglary scene to carry out an examination. In addition to fingerprints and/or DNA they will also be checking for the presence of footwear marks, fibres, and body fluids such as blood. If a window has been broken, then they are likely to take a sample of the broken glass for comparison. The suspect in custody will have their footwear seized in addition to their outer clothing.

The CSI who has attended the burglary will complete an examination report which will include details of any evidence recovered. A copy of this report will be forwarded to the investigating officer. If the CSI has recovered any fingerprints which may belong to the offender(s), then these will be sent to the force Fingerprint Department to be checked against the national fingerprint database. Any other evidence such as tool instrument marks from the point of entry or fibres found on broken glass would be recovered and removed from the scene to be safely stored at the police station. If the CSI recovered blood from the scene which appeared to belong to the offender (on broken glass or near the point of entry for example), then this would be swabbed and sent away to a forensic laboratory. If a suspect had been arrested in relation to the burglary, then a sample of their DNA would be taken from them (usually a mouth-swab) whilst they were in custody. This would also be sent to the same laboratory for comparison against the blood at the scene. If no suspect information was available, then the DNA from the blood at the scene would be searched against the National DNA Database to see if it matched anyone. A positive match would provide the name, date of birth and other details of a potential suspect which would be forwarded to the force concerned for the attention of the investigating officer. In urgent cases these searches can be carried out in a day or two, but the majority can take weeks. If there is no person identified from the DNA match to the blood, then the sample is retained as what is referred to as an 'unidentified crime scene stain'. It will be periodically searched against other similar outstanding stains and retained. If an offender is subsequently arrested and linked to the blood by their DNA, then the investigating officer will be informed so that they can take appropriate action.

The forensic element of a burglary investigation is a key line of enquiry and can help to identify and convict offender(s). It's important that the investigating officer and CSI work as a team and communicate regularly so that no information is overlooked. If there are a number of items which need to be submitted for specialist examination at a laboratory, they will have to prioritise submissions as there is a financial cost which must be met by the force. The days of submitting everything in the hope of getting a result have long gone, although there are likely to be many items submitted in the more serious cases.

For those who wish to write about the forensic examination of a burglary scene it's worth bearing in mind that there is likely to be only one CSI (unless the case is particularly serious) who won't usually be dressed in full white/blue protective coveralls and overshoes, but will wear a facemask and gloves to prevent contamination of the scene. The CSI will probably arrive in a white van (which may or may not be marked) and will be carrying their tools of the trade in a relatively small forensic case. CSI's are civilian members of police staff who don't have the powers of a police officer, nor do they carry protective equipment such as handcuffs, baton and spray.

CASE STUDIES – FORENSIC EVIDENCE
A heroin addict broke into a family home when the occupants were away for the night, but fled empty-handed

after setting off the alarm. The burglar was on licence for previous offences of burglary and robbery when he committed a further burglary in Usk. He cut himself after breaking a window at the address and left blood on the inside wall of the utility room. Detectives were able to link Junior Norris to the crime with DNA evidence from the blood he left at the scene of the burglary. He pleaded guilty and was sentenced to 16 months imprisonment.

Josef Ziga was jailed for 12 months after breaking into two houses in the Leeds area. He forced his way into an unoccupied property undergoing renovation and stole £600 worth of tools. Two bottles of cider recovered from the lounge were forensically examined and found to contain Ziga's fingerprints. In the meantime, Ziga committed another burglary, breaking a glass door to gain entry and stealing £3,000 worth of jewellery and electrical items. His blood was found on a bed sheet and pieces of broken glass on the floor. Ziga was arrested after he was stopped by police driving a car in Leeds when disqualified. The sentencing Judge commented,

"The offences were amateurish and not professional. The second burglary was made all the more upsetting for the victim because it was only two days before Christmas."

Serial burglar Antoni Dolphin carried a cloth with him to wipe away his fingerprints at the scene of his crimes, but was caught out after breaking into a house in Nottingham. Dolphin had 86 previous convictions, including 23 for burglary, when he broke into another house and stole a laptop and spectacles. The prosecuting barrister told Nottingham Crown Court, "He left the same way he came, climbing out of the window, trying to hide the fingerprints by wiping them with a cloth he had bought. But two workmen saw him breaking in and followed him after he left the property." Dolphin was found in possession of the stolen items and police later identified his fingerprint on the outside of the broken window. He was sentenced to three years in prison.

Intelligence

The investigating officer is likely to check through available intelligence databases to see if the burglary can be linked to other crimes or if there is any information which may help to identify those responsible. If there is a description and/or CCTV footage of the offender(s), then this will be circulated to other police stations locally and possibly nationally depending on the circumstances. If the identity of the person(s) who committed the burglary is unknown, but there is CCTV footage which may assist the investigation, then this footage may be shown to local officers to see if they can recognise the person(s) captured. The investigating officer may also arrange for a press release appealing for witnesses or anyone in the area who may have dashcam footage to contact police. This appeal may include a request for anyone with information about the burglary or those responsible to contact the independent charity Crimestoppers anonymously either online or by phone on 0800 555111.

People who give information to the police about crime in return for financial or other gain are now known as a Covert Human Intelligence Source (CHIS). These individuals, who used to be called 'informants', can help to solve crime as they are often part of the criminal fraternity or close to someone who is. A CHIS may be asked if they have heard anything about the burglary or 'tasked' to find out information such as who was involved or where the stolen property went. There are strict guidelines in place regarding the use and conduct of a CHIS, but they may well be able to provide useful information to assist a burglary investigation. The investigating officer may also carry out enquiries at local second-hand shops and other locations where property stolen from the burglary may have been sold or pawned.

Victim care

Burglary can have a devastating impact on victims and, in some cases, can lead to a deterioration in health and confidence. The investigating officer should regularly update the victim in relation to the progress of the case and refer them to other policing services such as local neighbourhood policing staff and crime prevention when appropriate. They should also consider external support services including Victim Support. If the victim is required to attend court as a witness the investigating officer should explain the process and make sure that the victim is supported throughout the court case.

Hopefully, I've been able to give you an idea of how the police will respond to and investigate a burglary. To summarise, here's an example from initial call to conviction.

Burglary investigation example
Mrs. East hears the sound of breaking glass and looks out of her window to see a figure climbing through the ground floor window of the house she backs onto. She knows that her neighbours are normally out at work during the day. She dials 999 and calls police, providing her details, the address concerned and an account of what she saw. The call-taker creates a police incident report on the computer and passes

the details to colleagues in the force control room. The offender is described as a white male wearing a red top, dark coloured tracksuit bottoms and a white baseball cap. The call is graded as Urgent as there appears to be a crime in progress and a local police response vehicle is dispatched to the scene. Due to the circumstances and the fact that the vehicle is single-crewed, another response vehicle is dispatched to assist. On hearing the details circulated on the police radio, a dog unit volunteers to make their way too.

The first officer to arrive at the scene, PC Aldred, confirms that the house has been broken into, but the offender is no longer there. He requests CSI attendance and remains at the scene until the occupier returns a short time later. In the meantime, his colleague PC West, has a drive around the local streets to see if she can spot anyone matching the description. This proves negative so, after consulting with PC Aldred, she takes a walk along the street where the burglary occurred to look for witness and CCTV opportunities. She speaks with a local resident who had noticed a suspicious black Audi car which had been driving up and down the street several times that morning and had been parked in the street earlier. The resident had made a note of the car index number which she gives to the officer who takes a brief witness statement from her. PC West carries out some more house-to-house enquiries before being called away to another urgent call. At one house, where there was no reply, she notices what appear to be CCTV cameras at the front of the property. When she has the opportunity, she updates the crime report with her actions and books the piece of paper containing the index number into the property system at the police station for the attention of the investigating officer.

CSI Beattie attends the scene and carries out a forensic examination. He recovers fingerprints from one of the panes of glass adjacent to the point of entry and on a jewellery box in one of the bedrooms. He also recovers some red fibres from the jagged edge of a piece of broken glass. Finally, he takes some broken glass samples in case they are required for comparison at a later stage. The occupier is able to confirm that the box has been opened and a quantity of jewellery stolen from inside.

The burglary is allocated to an investigating officer, DC Brown, who familiarises himself with the case by reading the updated crime report. He carries out police intelligence checks on the suspicious Audi which, although not currently registered to an owner, does have recent information that it is being used by a known offender, Turner. He has previous convictions for burglary and was stopped driving the car the day before. DC Brown goes to the scene of the burglary where he takes a witness statement from the victim. He also takes a statement from the witness, Mrs East, who confirms the description of the offender, but didn't get a look at his face and would be unable to recognise him again. DC Brown then carries out some outstanding house to house enquiries with a negative result. This includes the house with the cameras which turn out to be fake and not capable of recording. On the way back to the station he takes a drive around the vicinity of Turner's flat where he finds the black Audi hidden at the back of the block. Enquiries with local authority CCTV establish that the car was captured on camera close to the burglary scene at the relevant time. The footage is clear enough for local officers to be able to confirm that the driver and sole occupant is Turner, who is wearing a red top and a light coloured cap.

The fingerprint department are able to confirm that the fingerprints recovered from the burglary scene belong to Turner. The fingerprint expert phones CSI Beattie to inform him and sends a confirmation e-mail to him and the investigating officer. She also completes a witness statement and forwards a copy. DC Brown and CSI Beattie discuss the available and outstanding forensic evidence.

There is sufficient evidence to arrest Turner on suspicion of the burglary, but DC Brown is concerned that he may be alerted if police go to his address and he isn't there. The officer would also like to search the flat for stolen property and items connected to the crime such as the clothing worn by Turner at the time. He prepares an application for a search warrant under the Theft Act 1968 and goes to the local Magistrates Court where he presents his information to the bench. The application is successful and, after briefing other officers, they go to Turner's flat where he is located. He is arrested on suspicion of burglary. During a search some jewellery, later identified by the victim as stolen in the burglary, is found hidden in the fridge. A red hooded top and a white baseball cap are found on the floor in the bedroom. At the conclusion of the search Turner is taken to the police station where he is interviewed. He makes 'no comment' to all questions put to him. DC Brown feels that he has sufficient evidence to charge Turner with the burglary and phones the local Crown Prosecution Service (CPS) branch to seek advice. He discusses the case with a lawyer and e-mails the relevant paperwork. CPS recommend a charge of burglary and later that day Turner is charged with the offence. Due to the circumstances and his previous offending history, he is remanded in custody to appear at the next available court. DC Brown keeps the victim updated throughout and takes a Victim Impact statement detailing the way that the burglary has adversely affected the victim. This statement will be considered by the court prior to any sentencing. At the first opportunity, Turner pleads guilty to burglary and receives a 4-year prison sentence.

I accept that this is an 'ideal world' scenario, which unfortunately doesn't happen often enough, but I hope it gives you an idea of the police response to, and the investigation of, an offence of burglary.

2 in 1 burglary

A 2 in 1 burglary is a term used by the police when a person breaks into your home with the specific intent to take your car keys and steal your car. This type of burglary is also sometimes called a 'car key burglary' or a 'Hanoi' burglary (a reference to Operation Hanoi, a police operation to crack-down on this type of crime). They are often committed by organised criminals who target high-performance vehicles parked outside houses. Their ideal scenario is for the keys to be left nice and handy on view near the front door. On the odd occasion, a burglar who is looking for relatively small items that they can easily sell on, will be unable to resist the sight of the keys and may decide to also steal the vehicle, not only as a means of escape, but also to transport the stolen goods. These stolen cars may be abandoned some distance away from the scene or kept and used to commit other burglaries. In order to disguise the true identity of the vehicle, criminals may identify a similar vehicle and steal the number plates to put on the stolen car. They will then commit a burglary at a shop or supermarket in the early hours of the morning often targeting cigarettes and alcohol. The stolen car won't trigger Automatic Number

Plate Recognition (ANPR) cameras as the plates are unlikely to have been reported stolen due to the owner still being asleep in bed which improves their chances of escaping undetected.

CASE STUDIES – 2 IN 1 BURGLARY

Police patrols were stepped up and residents were asked to review their security after high-performance cars were stolen from rural areas on the outskirts of York. Several of the incidents involved valuable cars which appear to have been deliberately targeted. On Monday 5th November 2018 two daytime burglaries were reported in Nether Poppleton, one of which resulted in an Audi A1 being stolen. Overnight from Tuesday 6th into Wednesday 7th November, an Audi A3 was stolen from Wheldrake, and another vehicle was targeted, but not taken. The same night a burglary was reported in Elvington and suspicious activity was reported around a vehicle in the village. Home break-ins where a car is stolen are known as '2 in 1 burglaries' as thieves break into your home, take your car keys and steal your car. Whilst in your home they may help themselves to your other property too. Houses with high-performance cars parked outside are more likely to be targeted. A spokesman for North Yorkshire Police commented, "There are three very easy steps you can take to reduce the chances of becoming a victim of a 2 in 1 burglary – lock your car, secure your home and hide your keys. As well as keeping car keys secure, consider installing trackers in particularly valuable vehicles, as well as CCTV systems and house alarms in your property. Residents can contact their local Neighbourhood Policing Team on 101 for expert crime prevention advice. We can survey your security arrangements, and offer advice on keeping your home, property and family safe." Residents were urged to report suspicious activity to the police on 101 (or 999 if a crime was in progress).

A gang of burglars who targeted expensive cars across Leeds have been brought to justice after they bragged about their criminal exploits on social media. Specialist police officers built up a comprehensive picture of evidence as they investigated a series of burglaries involving the theft of cars valued in excess of half a million pounds. One of the group, Frankie Allwork, posed in front of a stolen £60,000 Audi A6 while holding a pair of mole grip pliers, used to break into homes to steal car keys. The image was sent to a notorious West Midlands social media account called Mr Dingers – 'dingers' being slang for stolen cars – where offenders anonymously show off about their crimes. Allwork's face was obscured with an emoji when the picture appeared online, but officers found the original unedited image of him with the stolen vehicle when they seized a phone belonging to one of his accomplices. A video had also been posted on the account, showing the suspects driving along to music in the Audi, which had been stolen in a burglary in Shadwell. The Audi and a £30,000 Seat Leon FR, stolen in a burglary the same night, were also photographed by the gang parked side by side in Gipton – at a location where tracking devices from other stolen cars had previously been found discarded. Phone evidence identified that Allwork had exchanged messages on social media with accomplice Bryn Kerry, talking openly about their crimes.

Allwork was linked to another burglary after his DNA was recovered from a cigarette butt. In December 2019, a £40,000 Mercedes, a £30,000 BMW and a motorbike worth

£4,000 were stolen in a burglary at a house in Rothwell. When officers checked for CCTV in the area, they found footage of the offenders arriving nearby in a car. One of the group was seen to flick a cigarette which landed on a garden hedge. The cigarette was recovered and found to match Allwork's DNA profile. He initially refused to accept that it was his DNA, but later pleaded guilty to the offence. He also admitted his involvement in a burglary in January 2019 where a £100,000 Mercedes E63 was stolen in a burglary in Scholes. The car was pursued by officers and drove on the wrong side of the road at speeds of up to 120mph without lights until it was abandoned. Allwork was found hiding nearby. Other enquiries by the investigating officers identified additional evidence that resulted in a number of charges against the group. Four individuals were sent to prison for their roles in a significant number of burglaries where vehicles were stolen. The head of Leeds District Crime Team commented, "It is clear from the way they bragged about these offences on social media that these offenders had absolute contempt for their victims and did not care about the harm they were causing. They each played a part in a very significant series of burglaries where people's homes were targeted to steal their high-value cars while they slept."

Distraction burglary

A distraction burglary is exactly as it sounds, a burglary committed by the use of some form of distraction. It is often carried out by more than one offender as this can make it easier to distract the householder. These criminals are often referred to as 'bogus callers' and are responsible for about 12,000 distraction burglaries every year. There are a number of ways that they operate and they tend to target older people who are often more vulnerable. The most common method is for them to pretend that they are from the 'water board', a term which isn't used by your water suppliers these days and hasn't been for some considerable time. They will claim that there is a water leak or contamination in the area and tell you that they need to come into the house to check the water supply by turning the taps on. One person will distract you in the house while the other takes a look in other rooms searching for items to steal. Sometimes the victim won't realise that they have been burgled until later when the offenders have gone. Those responsible will often look the part, wearing a high-visibility jacket, perhaps carrying a clipboard and in possession of a false ID card. They tend to be forensically aware and may wear gloves or make sure their clothing covers their hands when touching surfaces. When I joined the police in the early 1980's the 'water board' tactic was common, and it still is today. Occasionally, criminals may pretend to be from one of the other utility companies, the police, or perhaps the local authority. There have also been cases of unexpected visitors asking for a drink of water, to use the telephone or the toilet in order to get into the house with the intention of stealing something. These are all types of distraction burglary which, as you can imagine, have a devastating effect on the victims who often feel embarrassed and angry with themselves. The investigation of a distraction burglary will usually be carried out by a detective constable (DC) either from a burglary team or a general CID office. The investigation is likely to focus on house to house enquiries in the area (for witnesses and further victims), CCTV footage and forensic examination of the scene.

CASE STUDIES – DISTRACTION BURGLARY

A bogus Scottish Water worker tricked his way into a West Lothian home telling the homeowner, a man in his 70's, that he was there to sample the water. As he pretended to do so, an accomplice entered the property and stole a safe containing several thousand pounds worth of jewellery. A detective from Livingston CID commented, "Our enquiries have established that Scottish Water were not conducting tests in the area that day and we believe that the missing safe is linked to this incident." A spokeswoman on behalf of Scottish Water advised, "We're committed to helping reduce doorstep crime carried out by bogus callers. Anyone working for Scottish Water, or on our behalf, will always have a photo ID card. If we knock on your door, check the photo ID and follow our 3C rule: Card, Check, Call. Ask callers to pass their ID card or letter through your letterbox so you can check their identity. If you have any doubts call our customer helpline before you open the door. We can confirm if the caller is genuine."

An appeal for information was launched after an elderly couple in Wales were the victims of a distraction burglary. The incident took place during the afternoon of Monday 12th August 2019 in the area of Llay. Police say that three men were paid for allegedly carrying out work on a chimney, although witnesses reported that no-one was seen working on the roof. Whilst the victims were paying for the 'work', one of the men went upstairs and stole cash from a bedroom.

Sentencing

Burglary is known as an 'either way' offence which means that it can be heard in a Magistrates or a Crown court depending on the circumstances. A non-dwelling burglary with no aggravating features could be heard at Magistrates court where the maximum sentence available to the bench would be six months imprisonment and/or a fine. If the case is heard at Crown court, then the maximum sentence would be 10 years imprisonment which increases to 14 years if the building or part of the building concerned is a dwelling.

Burglary in Scotland

The crime of burglary when occurring in Scotland is referred to as 'housebreaking'. Housebreaking itself is not a substantive crime, but becomes one when accompanied by a 'felonious' intent. The two crimes which are likely to be committed are either 'theft by housebreaking' (where a person enters a building and steals something) or 'housebreaking with intent to steal' (where a person has entered a building with intent to steal). There are similarities with the offences covered by Sections 9(1)(a) and (b) of the Theft Act with two distinct offences which depend on the actions of the offender and their intent, although in Scotland both only apply to theft and not the other specified offences. For some time the maximum sentence for these offences was one year in prison on summary complaint, but in the last few years attempts have been made to crack down on those who commit this type of crime with a presumption that all cases involving a charge of theft by housebreaking, or housebreaking with intent to steal (or attempts to commit either offence), will be prosecuted on indictment before a sheriff and jury. This means that anyone accused of these crimes could face a penalty of up to 5 years in prison if convicted. Crimes of this nature in Scotland are recorded according to the circumstances as either dwelling, non dwelling or other.

Examples

➢ Forcing entry to private house and stealing property = Theft by housebreaking (dwelling)

➢ Forcing entry to garden shed and stealing property = Theft by housebreaking (non dwelling)

➢ A permanent caravan used to sell food entered and property stolen = Theft by housebreaking (other)

➢ Forcing entry to private house, but nothing stolen = Housebreaking with intent to steal (dwelling)

➢ Forcing entry to detached garage, but nothing stolen = Housebreaking with intent to steal (non dwelling)

➢ Forcing entry to secure wooden storage hut at a school, but nothing stolen = Housebreaking with intent to steal (other)

As you may notice from the last three examples, the felonious purpose is inferred from the circumstances in which the building is entered. In other words if entry has been forced and the property entered, then the inference is that the person responsible had intent to steal something from the property.

Aggravated burglary

Aggravated burglary is a criminal offence which is covered by Section 10 of the Theft Act 1968. It is a particularly serious crime which is committed when a person carries out a burglary whilst in possession of his/her WIFE (a mnemonic used to describe a specific list of weapons).

Aggravated Burglary – Theft Act 1968 Section 10

(1) A person is guilty of aggravated burglary if he commits any burglary and at the time has with him any firearm or

imitation firearm, any weapon of offence, or any explosive and for this purpose –

(a) 'firearm' includes an airgun or pistol, and 'imitation firearm' means anything which has the appearance of being a firearm, whether capable of being discharged or not, and

(b) 'weapon of offence' means any article made or adapted for use for causing injury to or incapacitating a person, or intended by the person having it with him for such use, and

(c) 'explosive' means any article manufactured for the purpose of producing a practical effect by explosion, or intended by the person having it with him for that purpose

There's quite a lot to get your head around with this crime, so I'll just explain a little about the wording of the offence and the meaning of the weapons which may be involved.

At the time

The moment an offence of burglary under Section 9(1)(a) is committed is at the point of entry, so it's essential that the offender has the WIFE with him/her when entering the building or part of a building with the intention of committing one of the trigger offences under s. 9(1)(a). To remind you, those offences are theft, GBH and/or unlawful damage. If that is the case, then the offender commits aggravated burglary. The moment at which a burglary under s. 9(1)(b) is committed is when the offender steals, inflicts GBH on any person or attempts to do either. If the offender has the WIFE with him when committing or attempting to commit either offence, an aggravated burglary is committed.

Example

Collins enters the kitchen of a restaurant which is closed, as a trespasser intending to steal property. When he enters he doesn't have any WIFE with him, therefore he has committed an offence of burglary under s. 9(1)(a). While Collins is in the kitchen he is disturbed by an employee. He picks up a knife (with the intention of hurting the employee if necessary) and threatens him with it. At this stage the knife becomes a weapon of offence which is intended to cause injury. The employee tries to detain Collins who stabs him causing GBH. This now becomes a burglary under s. 9(1)(b) and because Collins has a WIFE with him at the time, he has committed an offence of aggravated burglary.

Has with him

Some criminal offences involving drugs and offensive weapons refer to a person having possession of the item, but aggravated burglary uses the term 'has with him' which means that they will need to have some degree of immediate control of the item.

CASE LAW – R v Pawlicki and Swindell (1992)

Accessibility not distance is the test for 'have with'. The defendants were properly convicted of having a firearm with intent to rob despite the gun being in a car some 50 yards away from the offence. P went to some auction rooms with a complete robber's kit in a car, including two sawn-off shotguns in a briefcase on the passenger seat together with ammunition. He parked the car and went into an auction room, leaving the briefcase in the car, which was 50 yards away. P was joined by S who had arrived in another car.

Both men had keys which fitted handcuffs in the robber's kit. They were arrested and charged with having a firearm with them with intent to commit an indictable offence, namely robbery. Both were convicted and appealed on the grounds that they were not in physical possession of the guns as they were some distance away from them. The appeals were dismissed and the convictions upheld with the court ruling that a distance of 50 yards was sufficient for the purposes of the offence and the meaning of the words 'have with him a firearm', included if a firearm were readily accessible to the offender(s) when they were about to commit a robbery.

As you can see from the Pawlicki case, for some crimes the offender doesn't always actually need to have the weapon on their person. In the case of an aggravated burglary, the offence is complete if the person commits burglary when they have a WIFE with them, so an armed getaway driver who waits outside the house doesn't commit aggravated burglary, but the person who enters the house with a weapon does. It also has to be proved that the person(s) committing the burglary knew about the WIFE.

Example
Taylor and Lewis agree to commit a burglary together and approach a house late at night. Taylor is worried about being caught so decides to take a canister of pepper spray with him. He doesn't tell Lewis about his concerns nor does he tell him that he has the spray in his pocket. When they get into the house, both commit a burglary under s. 9(1)(a), but Taylor also commits aggravated burglary as he has a WIFE with him at the time. Lewis doesn't commit aggravated burglary as he didn't know about the pepper

spray, but if he had known, he would also have committed aggravated burglary.

Weapon of offence

A weapon of offence includes items made for causing injury (such as a knuckle-duster), adapted for causing injury (such as a sharpened screwdriver), intended for causing injury (such as a kitchen knife) if the offender intends to use it to injure, and items made, adapted or intended to incapacitate a person (such as handcuffs or cable ties).

Imitation Firearm

As the title suggests it doesn't have to be a real gun nor does it need to be capable of being fired. The interpretation of what constitutes an 'imitation firearm' is a matter for the courts. A number of items which look like the real thing will pass this test, but a person who pointed his fingers through the lining inside his jacket to try to convince his former employer that he had a gun during a robbery attempt, was found not to have been in possession of an imitation firearm and acquitted on appeal (R v Bentham 2005).

Police response

If the call to police is identified as an aggravated burglary, then the response should be graded as Urgent and appropriately resourced. It's entirely possible that response officers with standard personal protective equipment (body armour, baton, handcuffs, incapacitant spray) will be allocated to the incident, but wherever possible, they should be supported by officers with Taser and/or officers with access to firearms. Any available dog units may also be requested to make their way to the area concerned.

Depending on the circumstances, the response officers may be instructed by the force control room to remain in the vicinity and not to attend the scene until the arrival of suitably-equipped officers.

Police investigation

Aggravated burglary is a very serious offence and should be investigated by detectives (usually a detective constable or detective sergeant). They may be working from a general CID office or part of a specialist unit who deal with this type of crime. Depending on the circumstances, a small team may be allocated to the investigation, particularly during the early stages. The lines of enquiry will be similar to that of burglary (CCTV, forensic, house to house, intelligence), but is likely to also include passive data (ANPR, mobile phone analysis, internet/social media) with the focus on trying to identify those responsible as quickly as possible.

The welfare and safety of the victim(s) is always a priority and any ongoing risk must be reviewed and managed throughout the investigation. This could result in a temporary re-location of the victim(s) or the installation of a police alarm and/or other safety plans.

Sentencing

Aggravated burglary is known as an 'indictable only' offence which means that it can only be heard at the Crown court. The maximum sentence on conviction is life imprisonment. It is very rare for the maximum sentence to be imposed, but due to the serious nature of the offence, any conviction is likely to result in a term of imprisonment.

CASE STUDY – AGGRAVATED BURGLARY

A ruthless gang who held a knife to a four-year-old girl's throat as they assaulted her and her seven-year-old brother during a violent burglary, have been jailed. The five men, all from London, wore masks and gloves and carried firearms and knives during the break-in at an address in Essex in September 2017. They were sentenced to terms of imprisonment of between 18 and 28 years for aggravated burglary, robbery and possession of a firearm with intent. During the burglary the gang wrapped duct tape across a woman's arms and mouth, as well as repeatedly hitting a man with a firearm and a hammer. He was also burnt with an iron. The gang caused extensive damage and stole cash, jewellery and electrical goods before driving the victims to a field and leaving them there. Three of the gang had previously assaulted a man in his 70's during an aggravated burglary at his bungalow a week earlier. The gang members were jailed at Basildon Crown court in January 2019.

The Authors' Reflections on the Crime

Stephen Wade

I am fortunate enough never to have experienced the awful results of a burglary in my home, or even at a workplace. But as a crime historian, I do know that over the centuries in which it has been a frequent crime, it has caused a long and complex series of repercussions, both at the personal level, where the victim expresses the sufferings of such intrusion, and at the social level, in which the notion of the thief of the night is mediated in films and television dramas.

In my historical research, I have found that burglary is one of the most informative offences in terms of throwing light on the times, the social context. When I read the text of a statute, for instance, such as the 1861 Offences Against the Person Act, I can see that the paragraphs include bombs, child abduction and illegal abortion – all very current at the time as offences needing to be dealt with, but also needing to be thoroughly understood.

Consequently, for me, burglary will always be a crime through which I see the less plainly visible aspects of a Zeitgeist, a world spirit, the sense of the changing world around the criminal offence.

In all the case studies I have researched, particularly from the nineteenth century, when crime reporting was more widespread and more detailed, I have found that burglary always brings with it a drama as powerful as anything in crime fiction. This is because it is of such an extremely transgressive nature, with a penetration of ill-will and depredation into the very heart of domestic life. Especially when the criminal turns out to be a neighbour of the victim, the situation is extremely fraught with deeply vengeful and ill-natured emotions. 'One of our own' becomes a phrase applied to the perpetrator.

Even when, like Charles Peace, the burglar is a professional, and so is devoid of any sympathetic feelings or any local involvement, the fear is there in the crime-scene. A room is defiled, and the intrusion never entirely rubbed out. Paradoxically, part of this criminal assault may even be 'romantic' as we see from the fictional creation of Raffles, the burglar-hero created by Arthur Conan Doyle's brother-in-law, E. W. Hornung. After all, in more recent popular culture, we have had the adverts for *Milk Tray* chocolate, in which a romantic cat burglar brings chocolates to his beloved. Tell that to the victims of a real burglary.

What strikes the historian most forcefully is the nature of the 'with intent' adjunct to the burglary indictment. As the Maxwell Stewart/Lincoln case above shows, the 'with intent' is an extremely severe offence. It provides a close parallel with what will follow in this book, when we distinguish between 'robbery' and 'highway robbery.'

Stuart Gibbon

My earliest recollection of being affected by this awful crime was as a kid, when we came home to find that our house had been burgled. The mess and the thought that someone had invaded our privacy had an impact on the whole family and is something that I will never forget. Throughout my police career, particularly as a detective, I regularly witnessed first-hand the distress that victims of burglary suffer. A number of older, vulnerable victims never recover from the experience, items of huge sentimental value taken when they needed them the most. In recent years burglary has again impacted my family causing heartache and frustration. Whenever we write or read about the crime of burglary we should always remember those victims.

Bibliography

Note: the bibliographies are given with each topic in the book, but in the final 'guide to further reading' there is a more comprehensive survey of sources.

Books Cited

Cadbury, Geraldine, *Young Offenders Yesterday and Today* George Allen and Unwin

Cecil, Henry, *No Bail for the Judge* (Michael Joseph, 1959)

Denning, Lord, *Landmarks in the Law* (Butterworths, 1984)

Donaldson, William, *Rogues, Villains and Eccentrics* (Phoenix, 2004)

Eddlestone, John J., *The Encyclopaedia of Executions* (John Blake, 2002)

Gold, Claudia, *King of the North Wind* (William Collins, 2018)

Gregory, Jeremy, and Stevenson, John, *Britain in the Eighteenth Century 1688–1820* (Routledge 2007)

Hibbert, Christopher, *The Roots of Evil* (Sutton, 2003)

Irving, Ronald, *The Law is an Ass* (Duckworth, 1999)

McCall, Andrew, *The Medieval Underworld* (Sutton, 2004)

Moss, Eloise, *Night Raiders* (2019)

Richardson, John, *The Local Historian's Encyclopaedia*

HISTORICAL PUBLICATIONS 1974

Saunders, John B., *Mozley and Whiteley's Law Dictionary* (Butterworths, 1977)

Tout, T F., *A Medieval Burglary* (Manchester University Press, 1915)

Journals

Annual Register 1821 *Bill for removing capital punishment from burglary*

Constable T. E. H Jarvis, 'The Trowbridge Murder' in *Police Review* Vol. X no. 3 July–September, 1937 pp. 366–375

Other Publications

County Borough of Doncaster: Special Constabulary (No publication details. C.1940)

Legal Sources

Offences against the Person Act 1861 (Wikisource)

Online

https://digital.nls.uk/broadsides/view/?id=15199

This is where broadside documents maybe be viewed on the site
  for 'The Word on the Street.'

https://englishlegalhistory.wordpress.com/2013/05/30/
  history-of-burglary

The Times Digital Archive: 'Roscommon Assizes – Trial of the
  Ribandmen' March 9. 1820 issue number 10875 p. 3

Part 2

ROBBERY

"Rob: to plunder, to deprive, to carry off..."
Chambers' Dictionary

Introduction

In 1763, Parson Woodforde in Shropshire put this entry in his famous diary:

> *"Went with Dyer, Russell and Master after dinner down to the Castle to see the prisoners where we drank two bottles of port, and for wine etc., I paid 0.1.6. William Cartwright, a young good-looking fellow who is in the Castle for a Highway Robbery, drank with us with the last bottle and smoked a pipe with us, and seemed very sorry for what he had committed. We gave him between us 0.2.0."*

Woodforde, meticulous about his spending, had nevertheless given the condemned man some cash, no doubt for some strong drink before facing the noose. For such an offence, in Georgian Britain there was rarely any mercy shown.

Robbery, particularly in the form of highway robbery, stands in an uneasy place in the vocabulary of true crime and crime writing generally. This is largely because it conjures up images of Dick Turpin and other highwaymen. That image has been further transmuted by the romantic writings concerning such robberies. Yet there never was anything with the slightest hint of romance about a terrifying robbery out on the roads of our land.

Yet for centuries, robbery *per se* was rather hidden away amongst the statistics of crime. B. J. Davey, in his account of eighteenth-century crime in Lincolnshire, provides figures on various offences between 1771–1779. In only three reported robberies, the verdicts were: one bound over, one condemned to death, and one not guilty. In Davey's lists of offences, we also have burglary, grand larceny, stealing beasts, pickpocket, trespass and assault and horse theft. In other words, there was plenty of theft going on, but with robbery, in which there had to be a violent or frighteningly aggressive element, the crime itself was not prominent.

Similarly, if we look at sentences of death given between 1814–1834, we have robbery defined narrowly, and other types of theft listed, but now, in figures provided by Roger Hudson, the figures for these years for "robbery of the person, on the highway and in other places" are: 2,175 sentenced and 236 actually hanged.

Particularly in the narratives of crime between the Reformation and the eighteenth century and Regency, when robbery was a capital offence, there are thousands of accounts of the terror instilled by a robbery on poor, vulnerable citizens. Each robbery has its own structure and sequence of characteristics; when Falstaff, in Shakespeare's *Henry IV Part One,* gives the audience an account of his robbery on Gadshill, the language makes it clear that a robbery – an action given that name without any elasticity in the definition – struck terror and panic into the victim.

However, also in this period, long before Victorian legislation revised and clarified various types of theft, people wanted punishments to fit the crime, for instance, the great engineer and businessman Matthew Boulton, wanted the necks of the perpetrators when he was robbed. As Clive Emsley explains:

"Following an attempted robbery of his Soho Works in 1800, Matthew Boulton was determined to have the four accused executed on a charge of burglary. Boulton's son

*was most impressed with the eight-count indictment
prepared by his father's solicitors: it appears to be formed
like a swivel-gun and may be directed to all points..."*

We have our established usages of the word 'robbery'
but in everyday speech it is used loosely; in law, things are
very different, and as will be seen, in some senses it has
been a fluid concept among the general listings of felonies.

Historical Perspectives

In the centuries before the proper organisation of courts,
prosecution and law enforcement, the principle of payment
for criminal transgression was the order of the day. After the
Norman Conquest in 1066, for instance, William I wanted
nothing to do with capital punishment. He was an advocate
of instilling fear and giving crime a visible appearance in
society. In other words, he was for maiming and disfiguring
criminals, and also for extracting payment for offences.

In the Medieval period, there were all kinds of
punishments and a variety of courts, as explained in the
first part of this book. Yet there were also several ways of
avoiding prosecution. One example is the charter of pardon.
As one Victorian historian explains:

*"Charters were thus given to the innocent for money, and
to 'common felons and murderers' also, which had two
results: first, the number of brigands increased by reason
of their impunity; next, men dared not bring the most
formidable criminals to justice for fear of seeing them
return pardoned and ready to revenge..."*

Through much of the Middle Ages, serious crimes were increasingly seen as torts (wrongs) and these could be compensated. Also, as the King's courts developed under the Angevins, robberies and other serious crimes were offences against the monarch as well as against society. But there was anarchy aplenty. As the great historian Christopher Hibbert puts very powerfully, "... gangs of brigands, sometimes led by knights and often employed as mercenaries by powerful barons, frequently remained for years in complete control of towns." Hibbert notes, in his history of crime, that in 1451, "a gang of four hundred armed men rode into Walsingham during the sessions being held there and secured the acquittal of all their friends."

It has to be recalled that between the Saxon legal structures, in which a robbery was investigated by the tithing or hundred (as explained in the 'Burglary' section), and the later Middle Ages when the travelling courts of the assizes and the Curia Regis occurred, everything took place without a police force. The responsibility for investigation, questioning and arrest would lie with a variety of people, in a number of offices. These included the magistrates, the coroner, the sheriff ('shire reeve') and any local constable who worked with the quarter sessions. For low-scale offences, the summary courts dealt with the hearings and the punishments. But for robbery, murder, forgery, arson, rape etc., the people charged would be kept in the gaols until the assize judges met.

Consequently, when it came to robberies, the offences would either be subsumed into other categories of crimes, or there would be a special hue and cry to pursue and take the criminals. The notion of hue and cry needs some imagination to perceive. If, say, a gang of four people committed a robbery and a hue and cry was raised, then there would be the *posse comitatus*, gathered and commanded by the sheriff (as in the western films) and their task was to chase and take the robbers. In c. 1200 or even 1400, this would involve a large body of men, well armed, and the chase might cover a wide area. If the villains reached a town, they would find it very hard to hide.

This is why outlawry was general from early times, back to Saxon culture. If a person was banished for a crime and became an outlaw, he was beyond civilisation and he lost everything he owned and also any settled family he might have. There was a provision of sanctuary, but that was not a permanent resolution of the criminal's situation, of course.

This kind of reasoning opens up the very heart of Medieval society and law. Towns were small and vulnerable to robber-bands. They locked their gates at night and had a night-watch body of men. Yet they were vulnerable. They had no standing army, and relied on the local power-base, who naturally put their own affairs and property first.

Matters had not changed radically by the Georgian period, as in spite of the hard and repressive capital crimes in the statutes, the ubiquity of highway robbery and the highwaymen was logged in the literature of the time as well as in the court records. A typical instance of this was recalled by John Byrom in his *Private Journal and Literary Remains* where he describes an incident that happened when he was in a coach:

"We were half a dozen of us cooped up... it was very tedious, only we met with an adventure... for about half a mile or less of Epping, a highwayman in a red rug upon a black horse came out of the bushes up to the coach, and

presenting a pistol, first at the coachmen and then upon the corporation within, with a volley of oaths demanded our money – with a brace of balls amongst us if we did not make haste..."

Nobody was injured or killed, but Byrom uses some words which account for the serious conception of highway robbery. He says, "We had two women in the coach, who were so frightened that they got out their money, they had not strength to offer it..." The fear and the terror instilled was at the heart of the abhorrence with which the offence was regarded and explains why 'robbery' was so clearly separated from related versions of theft.

Robbery was thus a specific felony. As J. H. Baker, the legal historian, puts it, "... as an element in aggravation, it could turn petty crimes into capital offences." In contrast, as Baker adds, "Secret theft, on the other hand, was more an offence of dishonesty than of violence and was not immediately recognised as a felony." The crucially important concept was of, as phrased in Latin, *vi et armis*. This is *a forcible taking*.

We may rely on Baker again for further explanation: "... in 1473, a meeting of all the judges held that a carrier could be guilty of theft if he 'broke bulk' by opening a package entrusted to him..."

A similar differentiation exists with the crime of embezzlement. For a long time, the offence was hard to define and isolate in an indictment, as there was theft by stealth. The perpetrator had not actually possessed the stolen cash in question; in a phrase made memorable by its use in the television sitcom, *Father Ted*, money could be 'resting in an account' and in transit, as it were. But in 1799, finally, embezzlement was defined as a felony.

TWO CASE STUDIES

In the Georgian period, there are innumerable cases of robbery in the records of execution and in the 'last dying speech' documents. The reader is recommended to look at the site for 'Word on the Street' (see bibliography) for a sight of the actual original sources. One sentence from the case of Hill and Porter (1830) in Glasgow says everything about attitudes to robbery:

> They were "... *convicted at Glasgow Assizes of assaulting and robbing William Marshall, an old man of 76 years of age, in an avenue north of the city... paid the forfeit of their lives, at the usual place of execution.*"

His Bones Made Pots

The story of Spence Broughton ends in an anti-climax: a renowned highwayman certainly came down in the world – after being very much 'up' – on a gibbet.

This is a man who could have been a successful farmer, had he stayed on the right side of the law. Broughton had a farm bought for him at Marton, near Sleaford, when he was just twenty-two. He also gathered more wealth when he married a woman who brought money with her, but all this was not enough for this bad seed, a man who was, in the words of his time, a rake and a villain. He began by gambling, and he mixed with bad company, including a certain John Oxley.

With Oxley, contact started with a London fence called Shaw, and soon Broughton and his friend were taking on robberies. They were paid to rob the Rotherham mail, and the two men got to Chesterfield, from where they would begin the attack. Not far from Rotherham, the two men stopped the coach and there was only the post-boy driving. He was tied up and left. The robbers took the bag, but there was little worth having – merely one bill of exchange, though that was for a large sum.

While Broughton stayed in Mansfield, Oxley went to London with the bill. His problem was to convert it into money. In London, with the help of Shaw who had set up the job, Oxley saw that it was possible to do the business and walk out with the cash, in this case from a company in Austin Friars. After giving Broughton just £10 initially, Oxley found himself at the point of being pressured for more, and it seems that Broughton was pleased to take another £40.

Of course, now that the two men had come across a simple means of stealing funds, they were out on the road again; they robbed the Cambridge mail this time, and their difficulties began because a provincial bank note was traced – one of a number that the two men had been working hard to spend in order not to be traced. But they were traced after the energetic and sharp activities of a shop-boy. Some Bow Street officers traced the lodgings where Broughton was staying and, after a chase, they cornered him at an inn called The Dog and Duck. Broughton was taken to Bow Street. Their London contact Shaw turned King's evidence and he told the whole story of the robbery at Cambridge and of where and how they had dealt with and hidden the takings.

Later, the two men were examined again, and although the post-boy could not identify them, they were remanded in custody. The enterprising and wily Oxley managed to escape from Clerkenwell Bridewell. He disappeared into the night and we know nothing more of him. But Broughton was taken north to York. He was tried before Mr. Justice Buller at the Spring Assizes in 1792. There was Shaw against him again, and also a man called Close who had assisted in the financial transactions in London. Broughton was told by the judge that there was not 'a shadow of hope' of any mercy.

Spence Broughton was to be hanged, and also gibbeted. He was reported as having faced that sentence with fortitude, and he prepared himself for death, and was reportedly what the authorities would have called 'a model prisoner.' He died with four others on 14 April 1792, and before he died he said, "This is the happiest day that I have experienced for some time." The story of Broughton does not end there, however. His body was gibbeted on Attercliffe Common, not far from the Arrow Inn and there was a weekend like a local feast day, with his body being pulleyed up into position on the Monday morning. But some years later in 1827, a man called Sorby bought the land around the gibbet, and a few years before that, when some of the bones of the highwayman had loosened and fallen, the tale is told of a local potter who took some of the skeleton's fingers and used them to make some bone china items. One of these, a jug, was sold in London in 1871. Such is the notoriety of this Sheffield rogue that over the years, people have hoarded and preserved anything related to his story, and in one of the York archive stores, a piece of the gibbet is still preserved.

Nevison, Highway Robbery
William Nevison, a man most likely born in Wortley near Pontefract, and hanged in York in 1684. Most areas in Yorkshire like to 'claim' him as their own, notably in the burgeoning heritage industry, but what is not widely known is that there is a strong oral tradition that he was

active around Gomersal and Hartshead, and his most well recounted deed here was a murder, as he shot the landlord of a public house near Batley on one occasion.

Nevison's fame (or infamy) across the West Riding and also the South Yorkshire stretch of the Great North Road made him the subject of ballads and apochryphal tales; there is a cutting at Castleford called Nevison's leap and an inn was given his name. The song 'Bold Nevison' has some patently untrue statements, such as:

> 'I have never robbed no man of tuppence
> and I've never done murder nor killed.
> Though guilty I've been all my lifetime,
> So gentlemen do as you please.'

He was known as 'Swift Nick' and the name was won after a robbery at Gads Hill in Kent. He reputedly robbed a man there in 1676 and then made his escape on a bay mare, riding north at an incredibly fast pace, some say going from Kent to York in a day.

We know that his father was a steward at Wortley Hall and that his brother was a schoolmaster, and we know that the robber himself was married and had a daughter. His wife lived on to be one hundred and nine years old, dying in 1732. The oral tales pass on a complimentary view of Nevison, that he was tall and charming, and never used violence. The truth seems to be very different. A diary entry for 1727 recalls a memory of Nevison, saying he was living with a Skelton family – gamekeepers at Wortley. It reads, 'At the same time there lived with this Skelton Nevison, who afterwards worked in customs, but being out of his place, became a highwayman.'

He soon took to a life of crime, stealing when he was

only fourteen; James Sharpe, in his book, Dick Turpin, says: 'After being punished for stealing a silver spoon from his father, he stole ten pounds from his father and his horse, set off for London, cutting his horse and slitting its throat outside the capital in case he be suspected....'

There are paradoxes about this man who haunted the Leeds to Manchester Road around what is now Hartshead and the northern fringe of Mirfield was also once in service with the Duke of York at the siege of Dunkirk. Everything about him fits the description given him in the Victorian period when the myths were fully generated: 'The Northern Claude Duval', as Duval was the most famous of the gentlemanly highwaymen, and as the man whose life was once spared by Royal clemency.

He used to visit one of his girls at Royd Nook and would visit an old inn called The King's Head north of Mirfield; he would most likely make his way from that base onto the roadside and wait for the Manchester coach. It would be a good corridor to 'work', along what is now the M62 close to Hartshead. But the tale is told of him stopping at an inn in Batley while on these excursions, just to take a drink, and the landlord recognised him. The man raised the alarm, but Nevison was quick, and as the landlord came to tackle him as the robber was mounting his horse, the foolish man was shot and killed.

An apochryphal tale has the events at in Howley, and in this tale the landlord, Fletcher, tried to trap Nevison in an upstairs room but failed, and according to Victorian antiquarians, there was once a field near Howley Hall with a small stone on which was written, 'Here Nevison killed Fletcher, 1684'

The last adventure recorded is this: he was hunted and

was finally tracked down and cornered at the Three Horses Inn at Sandal.

Nevison was taken to York and hanged. He was captured by William Hardcastle, who was buried at Sandal church in 1696. Nevison had always had a reputation that placed him in the Robin Hood tradition, mainly due to Lord Macaulay's famous *History of England*, in which the great historian says that 'The great robber of the north of Yorkshire levied a quarterly tribute on all northern drovers, and in return not only spared them himself but protected them against all other thieves; that he demanded purses in the most courteous manner, and that he gave largely to the poor...'

Nevison, like Turpin, was most likely little more than a desperate man who had been an outlaw most of his life; it makes sense that, after concentrating on the Castleford and Wakefield areas where most travellers north would be easy prey, he would have to move west; the oral tradition around West Yorkshire plainly makes Nevison exactly the type to appeal to the later myths: courting young women around the villages between south Bradford and Morley, and having his bolt-hole around Mirfield, where the myths and tales are most widely told in the older local memoirs. True or not, it will not do the Bradford area any harm to have its own Dick Turpin character leaving a trail of murder and romance behind him. His fame had even reached Lincolnshire in the form of his ballad, as Percy Grainger, hunting for folk songs, found that the singer Joseph Taylor of Brigg, knew the song in 1908. In the end, the tale may be as much of an 'urban myth 'as that of the famous Spring-Heeled Jack who was supposed to haunt the London streets in the 1830s, 'a tall thin man enveloped in a long black cloak' said to be the offspring of the Devil.

From Victorian to Modern

Robbery in the nineteenth century, as with so many offences, underwent a cyclical course, having periods of intense activity, and other times when it receded. One of these periods really stands out: the variety of robbery known as 'garotting' and in the 1860s, a garotting panic took place.

TWO CASE STUDIES
Garotters
Up to 17 July 1862, there had been only fifteen robberies with violence in the city of London. But then a Member of Parliament, one Hugh Pilkington, was 'garotted' in Pall Mall. A new and terrifying crime against the person had been noted.

In its chronicle of November 1862, The *Annual Register* reported that there had been a 'garotte terrorism' in London and in the provinces that year. The word 'garotte' was beginning to strike terror into ordinary people and newspapers were selling on headlines about this new version of street robbery. The report expresses the crime in this way:

> *"For some years past there have been occasional instances of 'garotte robberies' – a method of highway plunder, which consists in one ruffian seizing an unsuspecting traveller by the neck and crushing in his throat, while another simultaneously rifles his pocket; the scoundrels then decamp, leaving their victim on the ground writhing in agony..."*

The popular magazine, *Punch*, covered the menace with its usual acuteness and dash; one cartoon shows some middle-class theatre-goers venturing out into the streets with a platoon of soldiers guarding them. It was nothing less than a reign of terror and it gradually became much more widespread than simply London's theatre land.

This 'modern peril of the streets' was first described graphically as 'putting the hug on' and it had its own jargon, the gang members having particular roles. First, the man called the 'front stall', a look-out; then the 'back stall' who was going to grab the booty and finally the 'nasty man' who would move in from behind to take the victim's throat. At the time, it was seen as a variety of crime that was somehow not 'British' and journalists tried to blame it on foreigners. It was often written about in terms linked to activities by Italian mobs. But soon it was realised that this heinous crime was becoming a speciality of the new criminal underclass of the expanding towns across Victorian England.

The terror even entered the realms of popular song, with lines such as

"A gentleman's walking, perchance with a crutch
he'll suddenly stagger and totter;
don't think that the gentleman's taken too much
he's unluckily met a garrotter..."

In the provinces the new crime began to take a hold towards the late summer of 1862. This year was destined to become a proper *annus horribilis* for good people on the city streets, and northern towns were no exception. In Sheffield, one of the first notorious garotters outside London was Edward Hall, a man who was apprehended after a desperate struggle with police. It was reported at the time that he was "the leader of a gang of ruffians who garotted and nearly murdered Mr Burnby, Earl Fitzwilliam's coal agent." He was cornered and surrounded, then jumped from a high window in his home in Sheffield, to escape. But in Birmingham he was grabbed and almost killed by a huge police officer who punched the villain relentlessly until he gave in.

In Bradford, the Chief police officer, Frederick Granhan, was about to be busy with this new type of robbery and his constables' truncheons were going to be needed more than ever. Characters like Hall began to appear in other parts of Yorkshire, and Bradford began to have its share of nasty street attacks by September that year. The streets of the city and the suburbs were indeed perilous at that time. A man was severely bitten by a dog in Grafton Street. He almost had his leg amputated. A fishmonger in Keighley was robbed in broad daylight on his way back from a lunchtime tipple.

A more serious attack took place at Jerusalem in Thornton, where Joe Savile was attacked and robbed by two desperadoes who came across their victim at Well Heads. The attackers, James Jennings and William Shaw, showed no mercy. Jennings took the man's legs tight while Shaw grabbed his neck, then they ripped his coat off and somehow he fought free. As the poor man ran off, the robbers shouted that they would catch him and 'kill him off'. Amazingly, though, the accused were acquitted because of lack of any clear accounts by witnesses.

Garotter gangs were not so lucky, and the full weight of the law fell on them. William Holes and James Lynas were in court for their garotte attack on William Dawson late on a Saturday night in Market Street. Dawson, an engine tenter, yelled for the police to help, and an officer came to the scene, to see the two robbers running away down Kirkgate. Holmes was trapped in an alley. Lynas was taken in Collier Gate by a detective called Milnes. They had taken a few shillings and a silk handkerchief. At York Assizes they were to pay dearly for that attack, with a long prison sentence and hard labour waiting for them.

In Calverley, on the moor, a Mr Summerscales was having his constitutional walk when he was set upon by two thugs called Elvidge and Hainsworth. They had used the established methods of one man behind to choke the victim while the other approached face to face, and they had taken his silver watch. But on this occasion, the victim could not positively identify the men and they lived to attack again.

Two hardened toughs called Lockwood and Murphy were one of the most successful garotting teams around Leeds and Bradford, and they became adept at the nefarious business They had a cover as street hawkers, one selling oysters and the other sold nuts. They trod the streets around the whole conurbation and were finally tracked down after an attack in Hunslet, though they had been active in Armley and Bingley. Murphy was the 'nasty man' and appears to have been extremely threatening and dangerous. It is not difficult to see how this crime would catch on in the criminal ranks and it reached the proportions of being a 'glamour' offence, in that in took skill, a brazen attitude and a total lack of fear. Lockwood and Murphy almost beat their last victim to death, and they took a trip to York Assizes, where they were due to suffer physical punishment and years inside.

The press began to speculate about how the most likely

recruits to the garotting craze were ticket-of-leave men. These were convicts whose terms of sentence had been lifted after good behaviour, so that they could go into society to work, though they were required to attend musters, just as today we have a licence system in the current penal code. A ticket could be granted after the prisoner had served at least three years. Penal servitude had replaced the use of the prison hulks in the Thames estuary after 1853, and men who had only served three years of a seven-year sentence could be released under this scheme. Ordinary folk started talking about all criminals as 'ticket-of-leave men'. The popular journals enjoyed creating this moral panic, making their readers envisage the local streets filling up with desperate and hardened criminals waiting to strangle them as they strolled to the Sunday band-stand concert.

All this led to the passing of the Garotter's Act of 1863. In some quarters people raised a glass to the villains because their actions had introduced extreme and repressive punishments back into the criminal law. In Bradford, the vogue had been just a small part of the life of a very violent and brutal community. One way of seeing this is to note that, while thugs were robbing in the dark streets, hundreds of men were gathering to watch bare-knuckle fighting, as they did at Cottingley Cliffs, when Laverty and Curlly fought on a Monday morning in this violent year. Two officers found the men fighting "near the bottom of a small secluded nook near Cottingley Moor, the ground around rising up in the form of an amphitheatre." There were six hundred people in the crowd, and the boxers were fighting for a prize of £10.

Everything about the city at this time suggests a community on the edge of reason and order. The women's refuge had hundreds of clients and even the traditional mummers' plays turned violent when fists flew on the doorsteps of good, honest people as the mummers' demands for cash grew too impertinent. There was even a minor scandal when some mill owners found themselves in the dock at the Borough Court. But at least there was no violence there: Thomas and Jeremiah Hall of Shipley had merely stolen £100 in a warehouse scam.

The year 1862 was a year of living dangerously in most English cities. In London, street crime was obviously at a peak of atrocious violence, but the north was certainly not exempt from this 'new crime.' As so often, *Punch* saw the heart of the matter, and in their cartoon, "Jones is not afraid of his shadow", they summed up the nature of this particular fear. The little man with top hat and umbrella sees the giant shadow of a garotter with a huge club on a wall as he walks along. But the good citizen in the picture, ironically, carries a revolver.

For sheer visual interest, a look at *The Police Review* reports is recommended.

Spark and Goldstein
In an article published in 2019, Duncan Campbell asked, "Whatever happened to Gangsters' Molls?" He gave a summary of the most notorious lady criminals throughout the last century and began his piece with an account of Lilian Goldstein. She was known through the inter-war years as 'The Bobbed-Haired Bandit' and she teamed up with Ruby Sparks, a colourful character who, amongst other feats of cunning and bravery, escaped from Dartmoor. The two were, as the media have reminded us, the British Bonnie and Clyde.

In 1927 Lilian was involved in a robbery at Southport. She was then charged with unlawful possession of goods. One report summed up what she was and where she fitted in with a group of men who were on the rampage: The woman was suspected of being an associate of three men now under arrest at Southport, charged with thefts carried out with the aid of motor cars.

In 1933, Lilian was convicted of theft. She was then thirty years old and her sentence was four months. This was small-time She had stolen goods valued just over £100 from a milliner's shop. But her real criminal career was still to come. She met and became close to Sparks, and by the war years they were busy all around the country, staging robberies. When Sparks broke out of prison, it was Lilian who took him in and hid him. The result was another appearance in court, this time charged with harbouring a convicted villain. Sparks was charged with being at large and Lilian was given six months.

As Alyson Brown emphasised in a feature in *BBC History Magazine*, these robbers and their depredations shine a light on some prevalent fears at the time: the motor car as used in serious crime, and of course, the involvement of women in crimes against the person and property, with violence integral to the *modus operandi.* Brown writes, referring to the 'New Women' concept as it had deepened in society in these inter-war years, the term being created in late Victorian times: "They ploughed new furrows in education, employment and physical activity, and embraced the latest fashions. But they also invited opprobrium – chiefly because they challenged gender roles."

This all happened at the very heart of a new type of robbery, for which a new term was coined: 'Smash and Grab'.

Contemporary

The law

Robbery is a criminal offence which is covered by Section 8 of the Theft Act 1968. The definition is a bit of a mouthful so, as with the offence of burglary, I'll show you the law as written in the statute books, then explain the offence in more detail.

Robbery – Theft Act 1968 Section 8

(1) A person is guilty of robbery if he steals, and immediately before or at the time of doing so, and in order to do so, he uses force on any person or puts or seeks to put any person in fear of being then and there subjected to force.

Examples

Lucas has been out for the evening with friends and is on his way to the nearest bus stop alone. He is checking the timetable when he is approached by Wilson who says, "Give me your phone and money now or I'll stab you." Lucas can't see whether Wilson has a knife as his hands are in his pockets, but is understandably frightened and hands over his mobile phone and wallet. Wilson walks quickly away, climbs onto a nearby bike and rides off. Lucas manages to track down one of his friends and calls police. Wilson has committed the offence of robbery as he has stolen from Lucas and, at the time, he put Lucas in fear of being subjected to force.

Mrs. Lyons has been out and is walking home carrying her shopping in one hand and her handbag in the other.

Thomas runs up behind her, pushes her in the back and snatches her handbag, before running off towards the town centre. Mrs Lyons is physically unhurt, but very shocked and distressed. Thomas has committed the offence of robbery as he has stolen from Mrs Lyons and, at the time, he used force on her.

The offence contains a number of elements which need to be present in order that a robbery can be proved. I'll go through these in the order in which they appear in the definition.

Steals
There cannot be a robbery without a theft, so if nothing is stolen then the offence can't be committed. The legal elements which apply to an offence of theft (Section 1 Theft Act 1968) also apply to robbery. One of those elements relates to a person not being guilty of theft if they believed that they had a right in law to the property, so if you owed me money and I threatened you with a knife to get it back, then I wouldn't have committed robbery if it could be proved that I had an honestly held belief that I was entitled to the money. There are, of course, other offences I would commit in relation to my behaviour and possession of the knife, but not robbery.

Immediately before or at the time
The force must be used or the threat made 'immediately before or at the time' of the theft, so if the force used or threatened is after the theft, then it won't be robbery.

Example
Lewis steals a bottle of vodka from the local off-licence

and walks out into the street. The owner sees him on the store CCTV and runs outside where he confronts him. Lewis threatens the owner with violence and then runs off. Lewis has committed theft as he has clearly stolen the vodka, but he hasn't committed robbery because the threats made to the owner were issued after he stole the vodka, as opposed to immediately before or at the time.

In order to do so

The use or threat of force in a robbery must be 'in order' to carry out the theft. Force used for any other reason would not constitute robbery.

Example

During a fight in a nightclub, Watson punches another man who falls to the floor. As he does so, the mobile phone he is holding drops from his hand. Watson picks it up, puts it in his pocket and leaves the club. Watson has stolen the phone, but hasn't committed robbery because the force he used against the man was for a purpose other than to steal from him.

Uses force

The amount of force used by an offender to prove a robbery has generally been left to the courts to decide, but it doesn't necessarily have to be a huge amount.

CASE LAW – R v Dawson and James

At Liverpool Pier Head, a sailor on shore leave waiting for the ferry was surrounded by two men, one either side, who nudged him on the shoulder causing him to lose his balance. As he tried to steady himself, a third man put his hand into the sailor's pocket and took his wallet. It was argued that the actions did not amount to the offence of robbery. The Judge left the matter to the jury to decide whether jostling a man to such an extent that he had difficulty in keeping his balance, could be said to be a 'use of force'. The defendants were convicted of robbery. They appealed contending that 'nudging' fell short of using force. The appeal was dismissed and the convictions were upheld. It was documented that it was a matter for the jury to decide whether 'force' had been used in this case having regard to the ordinary meaning of the word.

On any person

In the vast majority of robberies, any force used will be against the victim of the theft, but this doesn't necessarily have to be the case. The offence wording relates to the use or threat of force 'on any person' and not just the victim.

Example

Two men run into a jewellery shop and one of them grabs a customer and holds a knife to his throat. The other throws a sports bag towards the owner and shouts, "fill the bag with cash or he gets hurt." The owner complies and the two men make off.

Although the owner of the shop is the victim of the robbery, the use of force and the threats were directed against the customer. The offence of robbery has taken place.

In fear of being then and there subjected to force

In a case where force is not actually used, but is threatened, the intention of the person threatening must be to put a person in fear for themselves rather than someone else. In the example of the jewellery shop (above) the customer would clearly be aware of the threat and in fear that they may come to some harm. If, on the other hand, the offender had entered a bank and handed a note to the cashier demanding money and threatening harm to customers if the demand wasn't complied with, then the offence of robbery wouldn't have been committed as the cashier cannot fear force on behalf of the customers (R v Taylor 1996). In this scenario an offence of blackmail would have been committed. A popular example often quoted to police officers studying the law in relation to robbery, is that of the person who threatens to harm a baby in a pram if the mother doesn't hand over her valuables. The baby is too young to understand what is happening and can't fear for their own safety, therefore an offence of robbery hasn't been committed.

As you can see, the offence of robbery can become rather complicated when you start to look at the minutiae, but in essence, it's stealing something whilst using or threatening force. In the examples shown, if a robbery hasn't been committed for whatever reason, then it's very likely that some other offence(s) has been. The police will arrest on suspicion of having committed a particular offence and the exact nature of which offence(s) has been committed will be established at a later stage. The Crown Prosecution Service (CPS) will decide which charges to proceed with and the courts will decide the outcome based on the evidence.

In addition to the offence of robbery, there are other alternative offences which may have been committed. If a person tries to rob someone, but is unsuccessful, then they may well commit an offence of attempted robbery. If two or more people plan to carry out a course of conduct which would involve the commission of an offence, then they are both guilty of conspiracy. Two people who buy ski masks with the intention of wearing them to conceal their identity when they rob a bank will commit an offence of conspiracy to rob. They will commit this offence even if they don't have the opportunity to rob the bank as the agreement to do so will suffice.

Types of robbery

Robbery can be committed whether the offender is armed or not as we have seen from the definition and examples shown. The term 'armed robbery' isn't used by the police anywhere near as often as it used to be, when banks and building societies were targeted by men armed with shotguns and other weapons. During the 70's and 80's this type of offence was fairly common, but is now rare. This is probably due to a combination of increased security measures and the opportunities for some criminals to commit crime on the internet and in ways which may make it easier to remain unidentified. Robberies do still occur at locations which store cash, such as betting shops and other retail outlets, but a lot of criminal activity is now carried out when the target premises are closed, as this tends to increase the chances of those responsible being able to escape undetected.

In the last few years London and some other major cities have seen a sharp increase in robberies and 'snatch' offences, where the offenders target members of the public in the street who are using their mobile phones. These offenders are often riding mopeds, providing them with the opportunity to commit the offence quickly and making it more difficult for the police to follow them.

Jewellers are also sometimes targeted by criminals who

use weapons such as sledgehammers to break the glass and threaten the staff before making off with valuables. The offenders will often use a car or motorbike(s) to get to and away from the scene. These vehicles may be stolen or displaying false number plates.

During my time as a detective in the Metropolitan Police, I was attached to a 'Robbery Squad' with a team of other detectives. The team was managed by an experienced ex-Flying Squad officer as Detective Sergeant. We investigated all robbery offences committed in our policing area in north-west London. The majority of these offences were 'handbag snatches' where ladies had been subjected to violence so that their bags could be taken. The victims were understandably traumatised and quite often injured as a result of their ordeal. As is the case with a lot of crime, a relatively small minority of criminals tend to commit a substantial number of the offences. We did have some success, but were often faced with limited evidential opportunities to identify those responsible.

The changing face of robbery

A report published in 2019 has concluded that offences of robbery are increasing at a faster rate than in any other major developed country. The wide use of smart phones and cuts to police numbers are identified as two of the main factors behind the rise. The report from criminal justice consultants Crest Advisory examined robbery trends across Western nations and recognised a decline in the number of offences almost everywhere between 2010 and 2014. Since then, however, the crime has increased in five countries, including a significant 33% rise in England and Wales. A spokesman for Crest Advisory commented,

"It acts as a bit of a gateway offence into more serious violence, whether that's because young people are being asked to carry out robberies as an initiation into gangs or because they're paying off debts. The opportunity to commit robberies may be greater here than in other countries."

The report suggested that the increase may be connected to the availability of smart phones, often the target for robbers, with 8 in 10 people using the devices, higher than any other country. The Home Office believe that improvements in the way police record robberies may also have contributed to the increase in reported offences.

CASE STUDIES – ROBBERY

Three men are being hunted by police after a tourist was stabbed in the arm and had his watch stolen in a targeted attack. Investigators say the victim, a man in his 50's, was robbed in Berkeley Square, Mayfair in June 2019 when his £115,000 Breguet Tourbillon timepiece was stolen. Police have recently released CCTV images of the three men involved who have not yet been identified. A Metropolitan Police detective commented, "This violent robbery was committed in broad daylight, and it appears that the victim was specifically targeted for his watch." The robbery took place about a mile away from where a 20-year-old student was stabbed to death during an attempted robbery of his watch in December 2019. A man has been charged with murder, attempted robbery and possession of a bladed article in relation to this attack.

A man has been convicted of numerous crimes, including 14 separate handbag snatches, predominantly from elderly and vulnerable women. Michael McCann drove around Hertfordshire in stolen vehicles looking for victims before approaching them as they parked their vehicles. He would open the passenger door and grab the victim's handbag before making off, sometimes using force to do so. McCann was arrested in December 2018 following a police pursuit in Hemel Hempstead after the stolen van he was driving activated an Automatic Number Plate Recognition (ANPR) camera. In April 2019 McCann appeared at St Albans Crown court where he pleaded guilty to 36 offences committed during a six month crime spree. He was sentenced to 6 years and 11 months in prison.

A gang of armed robbers who held pub staff and customers at gunpoint during a terrifying raid, have been jailed for a total of more than 100 years. Those present at the HG Wells pub in Worcester Park, London were lined up against a wall and forced to kneel as the robbers, wearing masks and orange boiler suits, dragged a safe from an upstairs room. It later emerged that two of the 'customers' were in on the crime and had acted as look-outs. During the robbery a gun was held to the head of a man and another was stabbed in the thigh. The thieves tried, but failed to put the safe in the back of their getaway car, eventually abandoning it as they fled the scene. The eight-strong gang were convicted of conspiracy to commit robbery and handed lengthy prison sentences. The Metropolitan Police Flying Squad detective who led the investigation commented, "They carried out these violent actions solely in order to steal cash to fund their own lifestyle."

Armed robbers who attacked security guards with hammers in a spate of cash-in-transit raids have been jailed. The men, described by police as "brazen", stole

£87,500 during ten robberies in Greater Manchester and Derbyshire between November 2018 and January 2019. They were caught when officers spotted their getaway car and they crashed into a bridge, following a £25,000 robbery in West Yorkshire. The Serious and Organised Crime Group from Greater Manchester Police launched an operation- codenamed Mowbray – after a spate of raids on cash deliveries at shops and restaurants over a five-week period that featured 'striking similarities', including the use of hammers to attack staff. They were finally foiled after crashing the car, which was displaying false plates, following a robbery at a bank in Halifax. The four men, all from the north-west of England, were sent to prison for periods of between 17 and 21 years at Manchester Crown court.

Police response
The first report to police of a robbery will usually be taken as the result of a phone call to the Force Control Room (FCR). If the robbery has happened more than 24 hours ago, then it is likely to be graded as Priority or Routine. In all other cases it should be graded as Urgent. The call-taker will try to gather as much information as possible so that they can make an assessment of the risk to officers attending and the wider public. They should establish whether medical attention is required and obtain as much detail as possible about those responsible including descriptions, direction of travel and any vehicles involved. The call-taker will circulate details via the radio and create an incident report on the computer which will be given a unique reference number (see burglary – police response).

The level of response to the call will depend on the circumstances, available resources and the perceived risk. If there is any mention of a weapon being used or threatened, then officers equipped with Taser and/or Armed Response Vehicle(s) may be deployed. A dog unit, if available, may also be deployed to the area. These resources will be in support of, rather than instead of, unarmed officers. It's entirely likely that the first officer(s) to arrive at the scene of a robbery will be a uniformed response officer carrying standard personal protective equipment (handcuffs, baton, incapacitant spray, body armour). If the caller believes that firearms are involved, then the FCR may instruct local officers to remain in the area, but not attend the scene until the current situation is clarified and/or ARV's are in attendance. Those officers attending are likely to be in uniform and driving marked police vehicles. They will update the FCR upon their arrival and provide updates as and when appropriate.

If the offender(s) has left the scene a search of the area will be conducted and, if appropriate, a police helicopter may be called to assist. The deployment of this resource has to be authorised (normally by a police Inspector) and may take a little while to arrive, particularly if it's based in another police area or not airborne at the time. Any description of the offender(s) and direction of travel will be circulated to other units who will be searching the local area. If the identification of the suspect isn't known and there is a witness who may be able to recognise them, then the police may take the witness around the area in a police vehicle to see whether they can recognise the person(s) involved. Any identification may be as a result of facial features or clothing worn at the time.

The actions of the first police to attend the scene of a robbery are very important in making sure that evidence is secured and preserved. The actions taken, or not taken, by the initial investigating officer will dictate how successful, or otherwise, the subsequent investigation will be. They should gather as much information as possible from the victim and any witnesses and will prepare and submit a crime report. The scene of the robbery should be secured and a request made for the attendance of CSI when possible. Any CCTV of the incident should be viewed as soon as possible to establish exactly what happened and confirm the description of the offender(s). It may also help in providing forensic opportunities as it may show places touched by the offender(s) during the robbery. If there has been any contact between the victim and the offender, then consideration should be given to the swabbing of relevant areas and the seizure of outer clothing if appropriate. Any descriptions of persons or vehicles involved should be passed to the local authority CCTV control room for observations. The officers attending should, where possible, carry out house to house enquiries and look for CCTV opportunities in the immediate area and along any known escape routes.

Prompt attendance at the scene following the report of a robbery will increase the chances of catching those responsible and securing vital evidence. A well co-ordinated and appropriate response, directed by the FCR, will provide the best opportunity for a successful and safe outcome for all concerned.

Police investigation

The investigating officer for an offence of robbery will usually be a detective, either attached to a local CID office or a member of a specialist team who deal with this type of crime. It's likely that the investigating officer will be a

Detective Constable (DC) although, on occasion, it could be a Detective Sergeant (DS). If they are on duty when the robbery takes place or 'on-call', they may attend the scene as soon as they have been informed. This will depend on when the offence takes place and other commitments. If they are able to attend the scene shortly after the robbery, then they will manage the investigation personally and direct resources accordingly. They will be dressed in plain clothes, either a suit, shirt and tie or jeans and casual shirt depending on their current posting.

Robbery, by its very nature, is an offence which is usually committed very quickly with the offenders often spending as little time as possible at the scene. They may also try to disguise their identity by covering their faces with a balaclava, scarf or a mask. If they are forensically aware they may wear gloves. As with all criminal investigations, there are some common lines of enquiry which the police will carry out during the investigation. Two of the most important after a robbery are CCTV and forensic evidence.

CCTV
There are so many cameras these days that you are likely to be captured on CCTV at some point. If the robbery takes place at a commercial premises, then they will probably have their own CCTV system which may record internally and externally. The offender(s) may also be captured on local authority CCTV and on cameras belonging to other properties. A critical element of the investigation will feature the identification, seizure and viewing of any relevant footage. This process will take time, but the priority will be any footage of the actual offence itself. From this footage it may be possible to identify the offender(s) or, at

the very least, confirm details of the clothing and physical features. A person who commits a robbery in a shop or other business premises may wear a mask or other facial disguise, but will probably have put this on nearby, so there may be CCTV of them before they put it on or take it off, after they have made off from the scene. This is one of the reasons why a trawl for CCTV is so important. If the system in the targeted premises has audio, you will also be able to hear exactly what was said and identify any distinguishing features of the offender(s). CCTV is one of the most important lines of enquiry in a robbery investigation and can help in the identification and prosecution of the offender(s).

CASE STUDIES – CCTV
A man has been jailed after pleading guilty to the violent robbery of a jeweller's shop in Haringey, north London in April 2019. Andrew Elliott from Luton was one of three men who ransacked the shop, stealing trays of jewellery and causing damage. A female employee was attacked during the raid. As they tried to make their escape, two of the men became trapped inside the shop due to the door trigger switch. As he desperately tried to escape, Elliott's disguise of an oversized fisherman's hat and sunglasses slipped to reveal his full face. He was eventually able to get out and made off. The robbery was recorded on CCTV and provided clear images of those responsible. Whilst on the run, Elliott took extreme measures to avoid capture. He had two large tattoos emblazoned on his right cheek and neck in an attempt to conceal the tattoo already there, which had been clear on the CCTV. The black and white tattoo designed to cover the original tattoo was of such

poor quality that the words on the original tattoo could still be seen underneath. Elliott, who has a number of previous convictions for robbery and was on licence at the time of this offence, was jailed for 10 years and 4 months. The other two gang members are still at large. The detective leading the investigation commented, "From the onset of this investigation, I advised the public that all I needed was the name of the suspect, such was the strength of the CCTV. This was clearly the case, assisted by Elliott's botched execution of the robbery and his bizarre attempt to conceal his identity, which included his amateurish disguise to the garish tattoos on his face and neck. This dangerous and violent criminal was left with no choice, but to admit his guilt."

An armed robber was identified from his underwear by police when they went to an address in Burnley to question his accomplice. Jordan Haworth was arrested by police for a knifepoint robbery after officers recognised a band in his underpants from CCTV footage of the raid on the Shell garage in Rawtenstall's Burnley Road. Haworth was also found with a makeshift mask, fashioned from a pair of tights, in his pocket. Haworth's accomplice, Lewis Banham, was found wearing the same clothes as those shown on CCTV during the robbery. Footprints from trainers belonging to the pair were also recovered from the scene. Burnley Crown court was told that the raid was unsophisticated as the defendants had only taken one pair of gloves to the scene with them. Both men carried out the robbery within days of being released from prison for other offences. They were both sentenced to four years in prison.

Forensic evidence

All cases of robbery should be referred to CSI for consideration of forensic opportunities. If the offence has taken place inside a building, then CSI should attend to carry out a forensic examination of the scene. If the offence relates to a 'handbag snatch' in the street, then there may not be a specific scene which requires examination, but there may still be forensic evidence in the form of fingerprints or DNA available on the victim's clothing or bag, if recovered. The offender(s) may have touched items within the scene, climbed over a counter, shed fibres from their clothing or discarded a balaclava during their escape. These actions are likely to leave behind traces of forensic evidence. Even if the offender is wearing gloves it may be possible to recover marks from the scene which could be comparable to the actual gloves if they were recovered. Footwear marks on the counter or elsewhere can be matched to the shoes which left them, as can fibres from clothing. A balaclava or other face-covering can contain evidence such as hair and DNA to help in identifying the wearer.

Locard's Exchange Principle tells us that 'every contact leaves a trace' as, whenever a crime is committed, the perpetrator will leave evidence at the scene and take evidence away with them. Edmond Locard (1877–1966), a renowned forensic scientist, went on to say, "It is impossible for a criminal to act, especially considering the intensity of a crime, without leaving traces of this presence." The evidence, although often invisible to the naked eye, is always there, the challenge is to find and recover it. In cases of robbery, which is a fast-moving offence often resulting in contact between the victim and the offender(s), this is particularly relevant.

CASE STUDIES – FORENSIC EVIDENCE

Two armed robbers who stole money from a convenience store have been jailed after one of them picked up a beer bottle during the raid and left his fingerprints on it. Greig Andrew and Frankie Pettit used an imitation handgun to threaten staff during an evening raid in Dartford, Kent. But Andrew picked up a bottle of Stella Artois whilst in the shop, which was captured on CCTV. On the evening in question Andrew entered the shop and picked up the bottle before queuing at the checkout. As he was waiting, Pettit entered and pointed a pistol at the cashier, demanding the contents of the till. Moments earlier Pettit could be seen on CCTV loitering outside the shop wearing a hooded coat and black tights covering his face. Andrew placed the beer bottle on the front counter, then leant over and removed the till coin tray. Both men fled the scene, but forensic analysis of the beer bottle identified Andrew as a suspect and he was arrested three days later. He was caught near a car used by the robbers and was linked to the car through possession of the keys and forensic evidence. Black tights recovered from the rear footwell of the car provided a full DNA profile matching Pettit, who was later arrested. Both were sentenced to more than 3 years at Woolwich Crown court for robbery and possession of an imitation firearm.

A man who robbed a Brentwood store armed with a machete has been jailed. In February 2019, the robber, wearing dark clothing including a black balaclava and gloves, walked into McColls shortly before 10pm. He demanded money and made off with a three-figure sum of cash. Police officers searching the area and found a black balaclava with a white insert on the garden path of an address. Further outdoor searches revealed a black woollen glove on a grass verge and a set of clothing in a bin near some flats. The items, which matched the description of clothing worn by the robber, were seized by police. A forensic examination of the balaclava produced a full DNA profile from the inside which was identified as belonging to Matthew Page. He was later charged with robbery and possession of a knife in a public place. Page denied the charges, but following a trial at Basildon Crown court, he was convicted and jailed for a total of four years.

A convicted robber has been jailed after he was identified from DNA in his hat following a gunpoint hold-up of a shop in Buckden, Cambridgeshire. Charles Lee burst into the One Stop shop armed with a sawn-off shotgun and ordered terrified customers and staff to lay on the floor. Lee and an accomplice got away with more than £8,000 worth of cash and postage stamps. They were challenged by a member of the public who saw them leave the shop wearing balaclavas. Lee threatened this person with the gun, before making off in a white Vauxhall Mokka which was found on fire in a field a short while later. When officers arrived at the car they found a black and grey beanie-style hat caught in the barbed wire of a fence near the burning vehicle. The hat was forensically analysed and found to contain DNA matching Lee. He was arrested and later charged with a number of offences. Enquiries revealed that he was already on a life licence, having previously been jailed for robberies dating back to 1995. Following a trial at Peterborough Crown court, he was convicted of robbery and possession of an imitation firearm, for which he was sent to prison for eight years.

Passive data

During a robbery investigation, in addition to CCTV enquiries, it's likely that other passive data sources will be considered. Mobile phone data can be very useful in identifying calls made and received, text messages and the location of a mobile phone at a given point in time. This information can help to provide evidence to support a prosecution. In a serious offence such as robbery, this is a line of enquiry which will probably be explored. If a suspect is arrested, then their mobile phone(s) will be examined and the contents downloaded. The investigating officer will also request data from the phone service provider to see if there is anything which links the suspect to the offence. The officer will have to justify this request, completing an application form and obtaining the authority of a senior police officer (usually a Superintendent) before any data is released by the provider. Even if the suspect(s) uses a recently purchased and unregistered Pay as You Go mobile phone or SIM card which they dispose of afterwards (known as a 'burner' phone), the police may still be able to obtain data in relation to its purchase and use.

Automatic Number Plate Recognition (ANPR) cameras also play a vital role in criminal investigations these days. A series of cameras strategically located on our roads record details of every vehicle which passes them. Criminals often use vehicles to get to and from a crime and, for this reason, ANPR can prove to be a very useful investigative tool. If the police have an index number for a vehicle involved in crime, they can search the ANPR database to see if a vehicle bearing those plates has passed through an ANPR camera anywhere in the country. They can also put an 'alert' on an index number which will immediately inform police officers if the vehicle passes through a camera, exactly where it was and the direction of travel.

Robbery investigation example

At about 5.30pm Mr Watson is walking his dog when he sees a man acting suspiciously at the side of the local off-licence. The man is wearing a dark Adidas top, light grey bottoms and red Adidas trainers. As he crosses the road on his way home, he sees the man pull on a balaclava and walk into the store. Mr Watson is concerned and uses his mobile phone to call 999 and request police. He tells the call-taker what he has seen and then waits further along the road where he can see the off-licence door from a distance. The call is graded as Urgent and a local response unit is despatched with another unit providing back-up. A couple of minutes later Mr Watson sees the same man run out of the store and disappear out of sight around the side of the building.

At 5.39pm police receive a 999 emergency call from 'Bargain Booze' off-licence to report that the owner has just been robbed. A man wearing a balaclava entered the store, threatened the owner with a gun and stole a quantity of cash from the till as well as a number of scratch cards. The suspect had left the store and made off, direction unknown. In light of this report confirming that the suspect had been in possession of a gun, the force control room deploy two Armed Response Vehicles (ARV's) to the incident. All units are advised that the suspect has left the store and made off on foot. As the suspect has recently made off from the scene, a dog unit is also deployed to the area.

The first officer to arrive at the scene is PC Henderson who informs FCR via her radio and enters the store. She checks on the welfare of the owner, who is shaken, but declines medical attention. She advises them to close the store and obtains an account of exactly what happened, including a description of the suspect, which she records in her pocket notebook. She then views the relevant CCTV footage with the owner. It shows the suspect walking straight to the counter and pointing what appears to be a small black handgun towards the owner who opens the till drawer and hands the suspect a wad of notes. Just before leaving the store the suspect grabs a handful of scratch cards from the display and runs out of the door. There were no customers inside the store at the time. PC Henderson notes that the suspect, although wearing a balaclava covering his face, doesn't appear to be wearing gloves. She preserves the counter and till area and requests CSI attendance. She also asks for CID to be informed.

Meanwhile, the ARV's and dog unit are carrying out a search of the surrounding area. The dog handler parks outside the store, removes his dog from the van, and tries to 'track' the route taken by the suspect. The dog indicates along an alleyway between two sets of houses with hedges either side. As they walk this route the dog handler notices something on top of the hedge. He carefully removes it and can then see that it's a black balaclava. He places the item in an evidence bag and deposits it at the police station later. The rest of the search doesn't reveal any other items of interest.

DC Lloyd and DC Miller attend the scene and take witness statements from the owner and Mr Watson. They take possession of the CCTV footage and carry out house to house enquiries in the immediate area. CSI Douglas also attends the scene and carries out a forensic examination of the relevant parts of the store. A number of fingerprints are recovered from the counter area and the display cabinet containing the scratch cards. She takes elimination fingerprints from the owner and sends all prints to be searched against the national fingerprint database. On return to the police station she locates the balaclava and arranges for it be sent to a laboratory to be forensically analysed. DC Lloyd, the investigating officer, speaks to the local authority CCTV control room and asks them to look through footage from their cameras in the town centre to see if anyone matching the description of the suspect can be seen either before or after the time of the offence.

The following day, the fingerprint department contact DC Lloyd to inform him that two fingerprints recovered from the display cabinet containing the scratch cards have been identified as belonging to Rogers, who is known to police and has previous convictions for offences involving violence. DC Lloyd carries out intelligence research to confirm the last known address and recent information about Rogers. The intelligence confirms that Rogers has recently been stopped by police and was described as wearing an Adidas sports top and red Adidas trainers at the time. There is also anonymous intelligence, reported to Crimestoppers, claiming that Rogers has been 'bragging' in the local pubs that he has a gun for protection as he owes money. As DC Lloyd prepares an intelligence package in relation to Rogers, he receives a phone call from the local authority CCTV control room with some good news. One of their operators has spent a considerable amount of time looking at footage from the town centre cameras and has identified Rogers walking through the shopping arcade on the morning of the robbery. He is dressed in similar clothing to the robber (minus the balaclava!). DC Lloyd requests a copy of the footage.

There is now sufficient evidence to arrest Rogers on suspicion of robbery due to the fingerprint evidence and the CCTV footage, but due to the robber being armed and the intelligence suggesting that Rogers may be in possession of a gun, the risk of harm to others is classed as high. DC Lloyd has a meeting with the local tactical firearms commander to discuss a strategy to safely arrest Rogers. The agreed decision is to carry out a pre-planned firearms operation using armed officers in the early hours of the following morning when there is the highest likelihood of Rogers being there and the lowest risk to the public.

The next morning, following a briefing, officers attend the home address of Rogers. Firearms officers approach the front door, identify themselves and request that the occupants come out of the address. After a short time, Rogers walks out wearing only his boxer shorts with his arms raised. He is secured and arrested on suspicion of robbery. A subsequent search of the address reveals a firearm in the top drawer of a bedside cabinet, a number of used scratch cards on the kitchen table and clothing/footwear similar to those worn by the robber on the floor in the bedroom. Rogers is taken to the police station where he is subsequently interviewed in the presence of a solicitor. He makes 'no comment' to all questions which are put to him. Enquiries provide confirmation that the scratch cards recovered from his address were stolen during the robbery at the off-licence. An examination of the recovered gun by a firearms expert has confirmed that it is an imitation which is not currently capable of being fired, but is very realistic in appearance.

DC Lloyd feels that he now has sufficient evidence to charge Rogers with the robbery and possession of an imitation firearm. Due to the time of day, his local CPS branch is closed, so he contacts the out-of-hours CPS for a charging decision. He scans the relevant forms and sends them electronically following a telephone conversation with the on-call lawyer. CPS authorise both charges and agree that, due to the seriousness of the offences and his previous offending history, a remand into police custody would be appropriate. The custody officer agrees and Rogers is charged and appears in custody at the next available court. Whilst he is on remand in prison, a result is received from the forensic laboratory. A full DNA profile matching Rogers has been obtained from the inside of the recovered balaclava. This additional evidence is forwarded to CPS for inclusion on the prosecution file. DC Lloyd keeps the victim and witnesses updated throughout the criminal justice process. He also takes a Victim Impact statement from the off-licence owner as the trial date approaches. Despite the strength of evidence against him, Rogers pleads not guilty to all charges. After a three-week trial he is unanimously convicted by the jury of robbery and possession of an imitation firearm. He is sentenced to twelve years in prison.

Once again, an 'ideal world' scenario, but one which will hopefully give you an idea of the police response to, and the investigation of, an offence of robbery.

Sentencing

Robbery is known as an 'indictable only' offence which means that it can only be heard in a Crown court due to the seriousness of the offence. The maximum sentence on conviction is life imprisonment although this sentence is rarely handed out.

Robbery in Scotland

The crime of robbery also exists in Scotland and is defined as 'when a person has been physically assaulted, or verbally threatened or weapons have been presented or used, in order to gain or attempt to gain property'. There is also an additional offence of assault with intent to rob. Here are a few brief examples of when these offences would have been committed.

Examples

Person enters a shop with a weapon and threatens staff, demanding money which is handed over = an offence of robbery has been committed

Shop assistant is walking along the road on way to the bank with the takings. She is approached and threatened with a knife. The assistant hands over the takings and the offender runs off = an offence of robbery has been committed

Person deliberately knocks another off his pedal cycle and while they are lying on the ground the offender makes off on the cycle = an offence of robbery has been committed

Person punches and kicks another, demanding money from them. The victim resists and manages to fight them off. No property is stolen, but the victim sustains a broken nose = an offence of assault with intent to rob has been committed

Armed offenders enter a house and threaten the occupier, demanding his car keys. He refuses and is assaulted before the offenders make off empty-handed = an offence of assault with intent to rob has been committed

The Authors' Reflections on the Crime

Stephen Wade

For me, the lure of a 'true crime' theme is irresistible, and the word that follows close on 'murder' is surely 'robbery.' This is not difficult to see. If we think of the Great Train Robbery for instance, the story is immediately large-scale and high profile. Centuries before that daring criminal adventure, there were the tales recorded in the *Newgate Calendar,* in which robbers abound. The villain who stands out, beyond all others, is of course, Dick Turpin (real name, John Palmer). But two hundred years ago, the notorious *Newgate Calendar*, made Jonathan Wild the prominent anti-hero: 'Jonathan Wild – the Prince of Robber' – was described in this way:

"He derived considerable advantages from examining persons who had been robbed; for he thence became acquainted with the particulars which the robbers omitted to communicate to him, and thereby was enabled to detect them if they concealed any part of their booties."

In other words, he was a 'fence' and a thief-taker, and he was to become the eponymous hero of Henry Fielding's novel, *Jonathan Wild.*

But naturally, for myself, in reality (apart from in literature) the concept of a robbery is one of nastiness, amorality and violence. There is nothing romantic about it. When I write about a robbery narrative in a crime casebook, I tend to keep an objective view. I guess that it is hard to imagine being forcibly robbed if one has never actually experienced it. Byrom's account, above is the answer to anyone who sees Dick Turpin as an admirable figure.

In terms of researching the crime, it has to be said that looking at highway robbery in particular there is invariably a rare contemporary insight behind the narrative itself. For so long it was eclipsed, but later when it emerged and was dealt with in detailed reports, not only in newspapers, but in *The Annual Register*, then two elements come through. First there is the reliable business involved in it. Imagine how easy it would be, around 1780, for three armed men to loiter in the bushes and then ride into the path of a coach, weapons drawn. One man pointed the barrel and the other two took a side of the vehicle. It wasn't the Wild West.

The word 'robbery' will always invoke images of violence, but strangely, there is a mythic narrative in existence which revels in the opposite. This is typified in the alleged 'gentlemanly' behaviour of the highwayman, Claude Duval, who some myth-makers insist was a 'Hollywood Regency' gentleman *avant la lettre*. This has no relation to reality, but of course, the genre of true crime has its roots in the kinds of stories told by the pub fire on a cold winter night, when sensation was demanded, rather than truth.

Stuart Gibbon

The crime of robbery can have a devastating impact on the victims and those who witness events, whether the lady who has had her handbag forcibly snatched from her grasp, the shop worker who has been threatened with a weapon or the student robbed of their personal belongings on the way home. It is vital that this type of crime should be treated seriously by the police and investigated thoroughly.

The increase in knife crime and the senseless killings

on our streets inevitably add to the fear that law-abiding citizens are no longer safe to go about their business. Whilst I can totally understand this sentiment, we thankfully do still live in a relatively safe society, although the fear of crime often outweighs the reality.

My experiences with victims of robbery during a career in policing have certainly stayed with me. A lot of the perpetrators, sitting opposite me in the police interview room, had no idea or simply didn't care what effect their actions had on those targeted. As a society we must do all we can to make sure that the voices of those victims are heard.

Bibliography

The principal source for the mostly contemporary material is Blackstones Police Manual 2020 (O.U.P). For the historical cases, all cases are from secondary sources except where stated; the latter are from archive material.

Books Cited:
Baker, J. H., *An Introduction to English Legal History* (Butterworths, 2002)
Davey, B. J., *Rural Crime in the Eighteenth Century* (University of Hull Press, 1994)
Emsley, Clive, *Crime and Society in England 1750–1900* (Longman, 1996)
Hibbert, Christopher, *The Roots of Evil* (Sutton, 2003)
Hudson, Roger, *Hudson's English History* (Weidenfeld & Nicolson, 2005)

Jusserand, J, *English Wayfaring Life in the Middle Ages* (T. Fisher Unwin, 1899)

Wilkinson, George Theodore, *The Newgate Calendar* (Sphere, 1991)

Woodforde, The Rev James, *The Diary of a Country Parson* (Folio Society, 1992)

Reference Works

Cyriax, Oliver, *The Penguin Encyclopaedia of Crime* (Penguin, 1996)

Donaldson, William, *Rogues, Villains and Eccentrics* (Phoenix, 2004)

Glazebrook, P.R., *Blackstone's Statutes on Criminal Law* (O.U.P., 2009)

Articles/Essays in journals and anthologies

Brown, Alyson, 'Britain's Bonnie and Clyde' BBC History Magazine (Christmas 2017) pp. 60–64

Byrom, John, Extract from Private Journal and Literary remains in Jefferson,

D W. Eighteenth Century Prose 1700–1780 (Penguin, 1956) pp. 22–23

Campbell, Duncan, 'Whatever Happened to Gangsters' Molls?' The Oldie Oct 330. 2019 Blog at www.theoldie.co.uk

GUIDE TO FURTHER READING

The books listed in the accounts of both robbery and burglary reflect the wide span of interest in the topics. Obviously, the crimes figure prominently in the literature of true crime as well as in legal writings. Yet, if the reader wishes to know more, beyond our brief introduction, then these are our suggestions.

The internet provides the usual definitions and accounts of both crimes. The most productive sources online, for research, are arguably in The Times Digital Archive and in the British Library newspapers.

For reference works, the books listed above by Baker, Emsley and Blackstone are recommended. Also, Geoffrey Rivlin's *Understanding the Law* 5th edition (O.U.P., 2009) is very useful.

True crime also provides helpful information. Memoirs, casebooks and accounts of specific robberies will all provide amplification of our material.

There are also very scholarly works which provide everything necessary. For burglary, Eloise Moss's book, *Night Raiders* (O.U.P., 2019) is such a work.

For a fuller understanding of the law behind much of the foregoing material, a good historical survey is essential. For a very detailed and scholarly account, J. H. Baker is very helpful. For a more general and less demanding read, the book cited above by Hibbert is highly recommended.

Perhaps the most informative as well as entertaining reading for the two offences through time is to be found in the broadside ballads, *Newgate Calendar* narratives and also in the Old Bailey sessions papers online.

For the sheer force of dramatic narrative and for some less well-known classic cases, the reader is referred to some of the Victorian true crime standards, such as *Mysteries of Police and Crime* by Major Arthur Griffiths (Cassell, 1994). His chapters are each on specific offences, and these are: 'Burglaries,' 'Custom House, Bank and Kindred Robberies' and 'Garotte Robberies and Robbery by Stratagem.' Here the reader will find less mainstream topics such as thefts of art treasures, confidence tricks, and also insights into such things as 'the qualities of a bank burglar.'

APPENDIX

Disorganised Robbery: Two case Studies from Stephen Wade's case files

Robberies arguably go wrong more often than they succeed. There are accounts of incredible failures in the record books. On one occasion, a gang of reprobates planned to 'do' a post office. They planned everything very well, and on the day they turned up, tooled up in a car, the thugs ran towards the door of the targeted place. Only then did they see that it was Wednesday, and that was half-day closing.

HERE ARE TWO OF MY FAVOURITE, VERY TYPICAL DISORGANISED ROBBERIES

1 The Puzzle of Walter Rowland

Sometimes a murder case from the past seems to come together, in all its material aspects, with a lucid narrative; that is, details fall into place and an overall picture of the crime, defined by circumstantial evidence, leads to one obvious closure and often, one clear suspect. The great Victorian judge, Baron Hawkins, would confidently accept circumstantial evidence and thought that any deeper scrutiny was a waste of time. Today, we have complexity at every stage of an investigation, and what appears to be clear-cut on the surface, is in fact a pool with very murky waters beneath.

Such is the case of Walter Graham Rowland, a complex personality whose two alleged murders have provided matter for several book-length studies. But now, re-opening this cold case is arguably long overdue. The official record says there is no cold case: he was guilty and was hanged. But now, revisiting this challenging affair, the jury is required to assemble once more.

Walter Rowland was born in New Mills, Derbyshire, in 1908. The place is close to Manchester, and that fact is important for the case of Olive Balchin, dealt with later in this book. When he left school he had an apprenticeship in engineering, and was clearly a moody and aggressive personality, having troubles with employers. The army was often a suitable place for restless types back then, offering travel and a touch of adventure, and Rowland enlisted in the Royal Tank Corps. This lasted a very short time. Marked as being medically unfit for service, he was back in civvy street by 1927 and at that point his criminal career began.

Rowland seems to have been always on the restless, discontented edge of life, whatever he was doing and wherever he was based. He drifted from job to job, and in June, 1927, he committed his first serious offence. As we look back at this early phase of his life, it becomes an easy matter to see why in his later life he was labelled as a nasty piece of work. The truly mean and brutal streak in him came out in his attack on May Schofield, which led to his having a sentence of three years in Borstal.

The victim was to be his future wife but on his release he married another woman, and she was to die less than a year later, while having a child. Rowland had come back into the world, no doubt after the usual flow of supposed remorse and vows of being a different man. But that was not to be. There were deep-seated personality defects in him. Working as a labourer now, his name crops up repeatedly, reflecting a life of petty crime, but with hindsight, we look back at this time and see a man with extreme danger to himself and to others.

He married May Schofield on 5 September, 1931. There was formerly some doubt about whether this was the same Schofield whom he had attacked, but a comment made by a police officer in a press report was that Rowland had married a woman he had once tried to kill.

The couple lived in Mellor, in the High Peak. Just before the Great War, this was a typical, small township out in the shires, with the obligatory churches, chapels and local landowners with their considerable power. The petty sessions were at Chapel-en-le-Frith, and Walter Rowland came to know that place very well. At the turn of the nineteenth century the population of Mellor was 1,200 in the township itself, and 2,993 in the ecclesiastical district. In other words, nothing much happened there, and for a restless deviant in search of thrills, that was bad news.

Ironically, the place is just a few miles away from Wybersleigh Hall, which in the post-war years and the 1920s was to be the home of novelist Christopher Isherwood, another rebel, though not of the criminal kind. We know from Isherwood's life that radical changes were taking place around that area at the time, but Isherwood wrote about the area in a way which shows how the place itself might have made Rowland's temperament worse: 'The sense of weather is overwhelming. Every view is a watercolour, dripping with melancholy. The desolation of the nearby city seems to relate naturally to the moorland.' Rowland's parents were close by as well, at New Mills, and this area figures prominently later, during the trial in Manchester for his second alleged murder.

The drifter returned to society and raised hell. His great year in this respect was 1932. He courted a married woman and was rejected, so the result was that he drank what (he thought) was enough Lysol, in front of his wife, to end it all – he was wrong and he survived, and the next escapade was highway robbery. The report of the incident reads as if he had seen too many cop films or read too much pulp fiction. He apparently went up to a stationary car in which a couple sat and threatened to 'fill them with lead' – along with a fantastical tale about his supposed starving family. The man in the car either felt absolute terror or merely pity, as he gave Rowland thirteen shillings. This was all the cash he had on him, and Rowland left them alone.

Here was a man who was deeply disturbed and dissociated from society. The facts we have, when assembled and studied, present a profile of a sociopath with murderous fantasies and what Freud would have had no trouble in defining as a 'death wish.' Speculations have been made about his early life and his parents, but it is known that both his mother and an aunt in Scarborough did washing for him and cared for him. His mother was supportive through all his trials. There is no reason to think that there was any profound trauma caused by misery in childhood.

Then came the least successful robbery in my true crime files.

He was tracked down and was detained in Wallasey before appearing at the Derbyshire Quarter Sessions, charged with taking poison with intent to kill himself and with robbing the motorist of his cash. The press report of those Sessions stresses that Rowland's case was one of many and that 'crimes were prevalent in Derbyshire' and that offenders were 'to be severely punished in future.' Rowland's highway robbery was tried alongside several other cases of robbery with violence and breaking and entering. A certain William Izzard had been 'running riot in the district for twelve months. He told the court he had no work and was on the dole.

What emerged at this trial was that a nurse had saved Rowland's life after he took the Lysol. This stuff is a cleaning disinfectant, and became a household name during the horrendous Spanish Flu epidemic of 1918–19, but later – by the time in which Rowland had access to it – the product was promoted as a 'feminine hygiene' product. It is interesting, and perhaps enlightening with regard to Rowland's sexual habits, that it was used as a vaginal douche, both for preventing pregnancy and as a protection against sexually transmitted diseases.

The amount taken would have certainly killed Rowland if it had not been for a nurse who was sent for. The charges were indeed serious. Suicide or attempted suicide were felonies in English law until 1961. He could have been given a very long sentence. But the chairman at the Quarter Sessions said that he was dealing leniently with the accused, saying, 'If this had been an assize court you would have been sent to penal servitude, and richly deserved it.' In fact, his sentence was just twelve months of hard labour. He was a young family man, with clear mental problems. Surely the court was thinking of this, and thought that a short sentence and medical help were what was needed.

His situation in 1934 was that he was virtually unemployable, having form in the nick and a record of violence; he had a young wife and also a daughter, Mavis, by his first wife, who had died bringing their child into the world. At this point, questions have to be asked about why he did not receive help. He obviously needed some kind of psychotherapy. But of course, the 1930s was hardly a time when this kind of medical help was easily available, and certainly not for the ordinary labourer. There was no NHS of course, and consulting a doctor would cost. In Rowland's case, he needed far more specialist assistance than a chat with a GP and some tablets.

The criminal life went on: trouble did not follow him everywhere, as he made trouble happen. A typical misadventure, which reveals a lot about him, is his bilking of a taxi-driver.

He had got himself from Mellor to Stockport and there he met with a Mrs Burke, of whom we know little. He persuaded her to take a taxi with him to New Brighton. That would be a seaside jaunt, a madcap offer for some fun. But actually he was on the run. When the taxi driver, William Grimshaw, saw that he was not going to be paid, he took Rowland to the police station and there, Rowland told the officer on duty that he should ring Mellor. When asked what charge he was on, Rowland replied, 'Murder.'

Early 1934 was a pivotal moment in his deviant life. He had killed, although he denied it. The escapade to Stockport had been some kind of crazed, wild sprint away from unpalatable reality. He told strangers that he was wanted on a charge of murder, and his rampage through Cheshire and Merseyside now reads as a last-gasp panic, a fugue undertaken by a man desperate to hide his personality from self-acknowledgement and his social identity from the reality which had always hung very heavily on him.

2 The Cornermen

Liverpool has had its tough and determined gangs. A long way back, in mid-Victorian years, there was a troublesome regime of thugs known as 'cornermen.'

One report from the front, as it were, pin-pointed some robbers who were notably aggressive at the time in that burgeoning city. The writer knew Liverpool, and he told the wider world about the city's problem with 'corner men':

'Nobody could shut his eyes to the fact, after what had occurred lately, that there had existed for some time in Liverpool a particular class of persons who had become so well known as to acquire the name of 'Cornermen' whose business it had been to muster at the corners of streets and commit assaults, with a view to robbing and plundering unfortunate persons who might happen to pass by. Some of the recent assaults had resulted in cases of a terrible description.'

The writer was exactly right. Some attacks had ended in murder. Earlier writers to the papers had clamoured for the use of the lash against street robbers, even those who were no more than street urchins.

In the summer of 1874 a gang of these robbers loitered around under a street-lamp. Their prey was in sight: a young doctor, Robert Morgan, who had come to New Ferry for a shopping trip. As he walked by the gang, John McGrave, just twenty but an accomplished thug, asked him for sixpence to buy some beer. McGrave's gang was known as the High Rip Gang, and they had conducted a campaign of terror in North Liverpool. McGrave didn't like it when Morgan told him to 'get a job.' That was truly a fatal mistake. The gang set about him, and knocked him down. 'My job is taking money off passers-by!' McGrave answered. The basis of their terrifying business was to instil fear and then administer the brutal beating quickly and with sheer force of numbers, overpowering the victim of their hatred.

After that the attack became relentless, brutal and vicious. Michael Mullen, only seventeen years old, joined in with enthusiasm, and soon the two principal assailants were kicking Morgan along the pavement like a football. After a while, police officers arrived, but by that time, the young doctor was dead.

Morgan's brother came after them, and police were close behind. Later that night, the main culprit, McGrave, was apprehended, and the rest of the High Rip villains taken in the next few days. The whole bunch of thugs were teenagers; Mullen had tried to run away to sea. But they were taken into custody and faced a murder charge.

A death sentence was passed, but Campbell was re-prieved a few days later. He had a certain record of good behaviour, and that saved his neck. Even that was no easy task, however: a petition had to be signed, collected and sent to the Home Secretary. But the public sense of outrage was not only in the columns of *The Times*; Liverpool families insisted on the young men being flogged to death, as hanging would have been too sudden and merciful. Obviously, that was not widely supported, and expressed a gut-reaction to the sheer heinous nature of this killing.

The culprits were hanged at Kirkdale on 3 January, 1875. The violent leader of the High Rip Gang was terrified of the noose; young Mullen was, apparently, much firmer and resolute in the face of eternity. A reporter at the time noted that a point had to be made about the manner in which these young men had killed their victim:

'Three executions in one day will excite, it may be hoped, a salutary terror among the roughs, not only of Liverpool, but of the country at large. Of late they have learnt by an inaccurate but not unnatural induction to regard murder by kicking as different in kind from murder done by other means. They have learnt also to regard murders in slow time as different in kind from murders done at a blow..'

The 1870s were a particularly busy time for the two Liverpool gaols, Kirkdale and Walton. The latter had started operations in 1854 as a panopticon or radial idea. But the two gaols shared their execution shed for some years, the gallows being taken from one to the other. Kirkdale did not close until 1892. These young cornermen would have found the Kirkdale hospitality markedly stern, miserable and tough.

The cornermen episode provides significant evidence of the absolute terror created by youth gangs in an age of packed streets, dark alleys and 'no-go' areas for the bobbies on the beat. They were disorganised, merely a rabble, but their robberies and assaults were indicative of the challenges faced by the forces of law when juvenile delinquency raises to a level of a serious crime wave.

INDEX

THE CRIME WRITER'S CASEBOOK

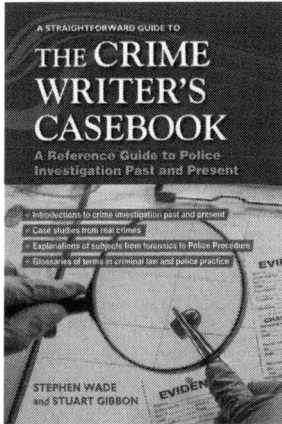

A fantastic addition to any crime writer's bookshelf!

Caroline Mitchell – Bestselling author

What a massive compilation of facts this book is – a must for anyone writing crime. Everything that you need to know, expertly indexed for ease of reference.

Pam Fish – National Association of Writer's Groups (NAWG)

This is a comprehensive and well-written guide for anyone wanting to write a realistic crime novel or a non-fiction work involving police operations.

Police History Society Magazine June 2018

If you're thinking of writing crime or crime thriller and wondering where to start, then 'The Crime Writer's Casebook' is an absolute must-have reference book. With case studies from real crimes, explanations of forensics and police procedure from leading experts in their fields and an understandable A-Z index of legal terms, it's every bit the straightforward guide it claims to be. Pick a subject you need information on, flick to the index, and you will find it. It's all there. Anything you need, you have it at your fingertips. Browsing the index itself got my writing juices flowing. I'm actually not sure how I managed without it. I honestly cannot recommend this gem of a reference book enough.

Sheryl Browne – Bestselling author

This book was recommended by author CL Taylor. One of the authors, Stuart Gibbon – a former DCI, has consulted on her best-selling crime novels for many years. This book is everything I expected and far more. Gibbon's in-depth knowledge and experience of policing alongside Wade's well researched and detailed references to historical crimes make this a must-read, whether you are a reader or writer of true crime or crime fiction. I am currently using this guide to help with the research for my debut novel. The information on forensics and police procedure, alongside case studies and facts about the law, is invaluable. Gibbon and Wade have packed an enormous amount of information into this guide, which is not only fascinating and insightful, but also incredibly practical and easy to use. I look forward to reading book two, 'Being a Detective'.

Samantha – UK Crime Book Club

BEING A DETECTIVE

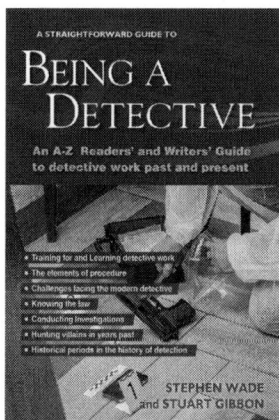

A fascinating insight into detective work, both in the past and right now. So useful for crime writers but also really interesting for anyone interested in police work generally. Simple clear language and great use of real life case studies to illustrate various points. A great companion to the authors' previous work, 'The Crime Writers' Casebook'.

Jackie Kabler – TV presenter and crime writer

After devouring 'The Crime Writer's Casebook', the first book by ex-Metropolitan Police Detective Stuart Gibbon and crime historian Stephen Wade, I was extremely excited to read 'Being a Detective'. And it didn't disappoint one iota. If you're like me, a crime addict, whether that be for crime fiction novels or those addictive true crime documentaries on Netflix, this is the perfect book to have on your shelf. It's bursting with information, everything you could possibly want to know is in these books.

Ronnie Turner – Author and Book Blogger

There are no words to describe the marvellousness of this book. It's a must asset for the crime writer. It gives a wonderful insight into the world of detectives and the difficult job they do. I felt having both authors in my living room as if they were present narrating me their special skills. A wonderful work full of technicalities which are a must-know for the writer who wishes to give a plausible brushing on his work. It's the second co-operation between the authors, after their book "The Crime Writer's Casebook" and I was amazed by the different perspectives and new information I got. I highly recommend it.

FloBell (reviewed in Germany)

I cannot stress how useful and informative this book is! As a crime writer, I keep it close at hand and use it often. I would definitely recommend it to anyone interested in the way police operate, writers of crime or aspiring crime writers. I love this book and it's a good way of ensuring that your work has an authentic air about it.

Griffy

A brilliant follow up book with even more amazing inside detail on being a detective. An essential part of any crime or thriller writer's library.

MR